R(

MW00943780

Lock Down Publications

Presents

Boss'N Up

A Novel by Royal Nicole

1

First Edition August 2014
Printed in the United States of America

Lock Down Publications
Email: tha_raven08@yahoo.com
Facebook: Royal Nicole
Cover design and layout by: Dynasty Cover Me Services
Book interior design by: April Green
Edited by: Mia Rucker

Royal Nicole

Chapter 1

"A'ight, it looks like all of our bread and bricks are in order," Yaseer said to the Torture Crew as they finished counting up their cash and dope. Bricks of cocaine and bands of money was stacked neatly on the table in front of them. "Is everyone cool with everything we just discussed?" he asked.

Six heads nodded up and down in unison. Yaseer took a moment to look around the oval shaped room at everyone's faces, making sure that their unanimous approval was genuine. They were doing big things now and success could easily breed envy.

Convinced that there was no hidden hate on his team, he said, "A'ight, bet. Now that we're done conducting business, it's time to kick back and enjoy the fruits of our labor. Let's meet up at Club A1 to chill, spark something and have a few shots. We can meet there at eleven. That gives us three hours to handle our personal B.I."

"Shoot, you might wanna say midnight. You know pretty boy swag over there takes five hours to get dressed," London said while nodding her head in Liam's direction.

Everyone burst out laughing as they all stood and grabbed their belongings off of the crystal clear circular shaped table.

"You just mad cause yo ass can't get none of this pretty nigga's dick," Liam said with a smirk and walked out of the building which they called the Chambers.

London stood there with a salty expression plastered across her face because Liam had just hit the nail on the head. *It's cool tho', I got something for him,* she thought to herself. She threw on her pea coat and exited out of the black double doors of the conference room, then out of the chambers, the same way Liam had just exited.

"I wish those two would just fuck and get the shit over and done with," Paris said as she walked over to Yaseer.

"Why? So you can talk shit when he hit it and leave her walking around stuck on stupid," Yaseer responded with a smirk while engulfing Paris into his 6'2", 240lb frame as he bent down to give her a kiss. It was only supposed to be a quick peck, but as usual the only thing ever quick between the two of them was their gun hands, trigger fingers, and money.

"Hhmm, hhmm." Kai'yan cleared his throat, subtly reminding them that they weren't alone just yet.

Yaseer lifted his head smiling. He knew Kai'yan couldn't stand to see mofos acting as though they were ready to get their freak on in front of him.

"Damn, son, did you clean shorty's tonsils good enough?" Kai'yan asked sarcastically.

"Hell yeah, I dry cleaned those mofos so good, my name should be Mr. Clean," Yaseer replied.

Kai'yan just shook his head. He knew Paris

had his boy sprung.

"A'ight, son, I'ma check y'all later at the club. Come on E 'fore these two start tryna hang on shit like it's a fuckin' Mimi pole," Kai'yan cracked as he started walking toward the door with Ezra in tow.

"Yan a damn mess," Paris said to Yaseer.

"Ain't he though? That nigga will kill a fool in a heartbeat but can't stand to see nobody kissing in front of him. My boy a fuckin' flight."

"He damn sure is," she agreed.

"Come on, bae, 'cause you know yo ass take forever to get dressed, too," Yaseer said, as he grabbed Paris' hand.

The couple walked hand in hand out of the conference room, down the hall to the exit, bypassing the numbered doors.

Yaseer opened the front passenger door of his all black Yukon XL. He waited for Paris to get settled in then he walked around to the driver's side, hopped in and started up the engine. He threw in

Rich Homie Quan's *They Don't Know* as he sped off, bobbing his head and singing the lyrics.

"And I'm the future nigga, I see your past/ who the fuck told you I wanna be your ass/ with these diamonds looking like water, boy I got Nemo mad."

Paris sat watching her man as he drove. Every time she looked at him when he was in the zone like that, it turned her on. It was just something about his swag that kept her hormones going ham.

Yaseer looked over at Paris. Shawty was looking at him like she was ready for the D. He smirked and shook his head side to side. *Yep, we're going to be late.* Yaseer wasn't about to complain, his boo could get it any place, any time. She turned him the fuck on with her sexiness, and her loyalty added to her desirability.

Glancing over at her before returning his eyes back to the road, Yaseer's mind flashed back three years to the time Paris had taken a gun charge for him.

Yaseer had taken Paris downtown to the Epicenter to catch a movie and then rented a hotel room for them at the Marriott. Back then he was hustling small time, selling weed, guns, crack, and pretty much whatever he could get his hands on to provide for him and Paris. He had decided to take a night off and spend time with her.

The next day they were on their way back to their apartment when Charlotte Mecklenburg's boys in blue got behind them and started flashing those dreaded red, white, and blue lights.

Yaseer looked over at Paris when something caught his eye. He had forgotten he had his gun on him and didn't have time to hide it before the cop approached his car. He'd already had his share of felonious cases, ranging from simple possession of drugs to assault, so the last thing he needed was a gun charge. The judge had already told him that the next time he appeared before him he would be going away for a long while.

Paris' eyes spotted the gun just like Yaseer's had. She had been there when the judge had said those words to him. She grabbed his hand as she watched the cop approach the driver's side and mouthed the word, "No."

Yaseer knew what she was saying. She had no charges on her record so it wouldn't be as bad for her as it would be for him. She would do a maximum of two years, but he was far from comfortable with that shit. The cop knocked at his window. Yaseer's attitude was turned up to the max as he rolled the window down.

"Sir, do you know why I stopped you?" the officer asked him.

"No, sir, I don't."

"Your brake light appears to be out," the officer replied while peeking inside of the car and spotting the butt of Yaseer's gun.

"Officer, I didn't even realize they were out." Yaseer replied, trying to be cordial even though on the inside he was ready to spaz out on the

short, balding man.

*"Sir, could you step out of the car, please?"
he asked while taking a step back so Yaseer could
open the door.*

*Yaseer stepped out of the car straight
muggin' the officer. He was as hot as fish grease at
a fish fry on a summer's day in the 'A'. The thought
of Paris taking a case for him was tearing his heart
to pieces and making him mad all at the same time.
He could literally feel his world being torn apart.
He already knew what was about to happen, but he
was far from emotionally prepared for it.*

*"Put your hands up and turn around,
please," the cop told him as he walked over to him
and began searching him from head to toe.*

*It was a good thing that he didn't have
anything on him.*

*"Sir, I'm going to have to search your car.
Ma'am, I need you to step out of the vehicle as
well," the officer said looking at Paris.*

She got out of the car just as calmly as could

be, like she didn't have a care in the world. The officer had her to do the same as Yaseer had done and then he proceeded to search the car.

He searched the car from top to bottom and the only thing he could pull out was Yaseer's gun. Yaseer figured the cop was hoping he would find drugs or something.

"Sir, is this gun registered?" the cop asked.

"No, it's not. It's my gun officer," Paris said before he could respond.

After that, it seemed like everything else was a blur. Before he knew it, Paris was getting cuffed.

Time and court dates flew by. The thing that hurt him the most was when he heard the judge tell his girl that the State of North Carolina was sentencing her to two years at North Carolina Correctional Institution for Women. But one of the happiest days in his life was when Paris walked out from behind those prison gates and ran jumped in his arms.

"Damn, we've come a long way," Yaseer said as they pulled into the driveway of their abode.

*****

Two and a half hours later, Yaseer sat on the edge of his California King sized bed watching Paris get dressed. He glanced down at his watch. It was a quarter 'til eleven and they still had yet to leave to go meet up with the crew. He couldn't even get mad at Paris because he had hemmed her up against the wall as soon as they had gotten inside, but damn he hated to be late.

"Damn, ma, if you don't come on. Everybody's at A1 waiting on us. You know I hate being late," Yaseer said, looking at her while trying to conceal his irritation. *I swear her ass got to know two weeks in advance that we going somewhere in order for her to be ready and on time,* he thought and shook his head.

"I'm comin'. Dang, I swear you stay rushing me," Paris said, peering at Yaseer in the vanity mirror with the most beautiful hazel eyes he had ever seen.

"That's 'cause your ass stay taking forever when it's time to go somewhere."

"You can't rush perfection, bae. Plus, it only takes fifteen minutes to get there. They still gon' be poppin' bottles when we get there so stop trippin'," she responded with sass.

"It's 10:55PM now. By the time we get there, only two people are going to be there. You and me," Yaseer spat. He was agitated because they were wasting time going back and forth with one another.

He was about ten good seconds away from saying, *Fuck it, we ain't going nowhere.*

"You are so fucking dramatic," Paris remarked while throwing on her thick, black leather jacket and gloves to block out the cool, brisk winter breeze of February.

"Well, someone's gotta be since it looks like that's the only excitement we will see tonight,"

Yaseer responded while standing up, grabbing his leather jacket, and pulling it over his black tee that showed off his well-defined biceps and pecs. He grabbed his NY fitted and placed it over his smooth circular waves.

Checking himself out in the mirror one last time to make sure his gear looked fly, Yaseer fixed his True Religion jeans to make sure they were sagging just right, just enough so he wouldn't be walking around looking like a square.

Paris handed him his Glock which he secured in the small of his back after making sure it was locked and loaded.

"Come on, smart ass. You were rushing me so let's go. Watch, we're going to be the first two people to arrive."

Yaseer shook his head. *I swear ma is a fuckin' trip, but that's why I love her.* "Yo ass got jokes, huh?" he said with a smirk. "Come on, snail," he cracked and then grabbed his car keys.

"When you trying to get some cutty, I'm

going to make sure to remember to move as slow as a snail," Paris replied as she checked to make sure that all of the lights and electrical devices in the house were turned off.

"Try that shit if you want to and see what happens. Bet I will have ya on ya Keith Sweat shit, straight begging on ya hands and knees," Yaseer said as they left out.

Paris didn't even respond, she knew he was telling the truth and nothing but the truth when he said he would have her begging. He knew just how to get her to the point of damn near groveling.

Chapter 2

Fifteen minutes later, Yaseer pulled up to Club A1 in his all-black 2014 Dodge Charger. He had it laced with black 22" rims, tinted windows, and the system in it was ridiculous. His crew was just getting there as well, so they weren't too far behind in time.

They all parked their cars, got out, exchanged greetings and then followed Yaseer and Paris to the entrance. They strolled past the long line into the club. TTC was in full effect.

Yaseer and Paris stepped in the club hand-in-hand, looking fly as fuck. They were dripping in diamonds. Yaseer looked over at his woman through the lenses of his Ray Ban cop shades. His girl looked sexy as hell rocking her short, all-black Chanel dress that showed off her back as well as hugged her curves. Her Red Bottom stilettos and TTC chain completed the ensemble. She had styled her hair just the way he liked it, bone straight and flowing down her back with a part in the middle. Yaseer was ready to back her up against the nearest wall and get a taste of her again.

He refocused his attention and peeped his crew. They were the shit and they knew it.

Every single one of them was packing heat. Their crew was tighter than a small thong in the crack of a five-hundred-pound woman's behind. Nobody was fucking with them unless they wanted to be tomorrow's news headline.

As soon as the deejay spotted the crew, he threw on their anthem, *Bossin' Up* by Kid Ink featuring French Montana and A$AP Ferg. Mofos everywhere automatically knew when they heard that shit who was in the fuckin' building.

TTC walked through the club to their VIP section. Once everyone was settled, Yaseer bent down to whisper in Paris' ear that he was about to use the restroom and would be right back. He was almost to his destination when someone he would have rather not seen tonight blocked his path.

"Now I see why yo ass ain't been returning my damn phone calls. You too busy up that bitch's dumb ass."

Yaseer's anger spiked like a hundred and four fever. Before his beautiful distraction could utter another word, he took her by her arm and pulled her off to the side into a corner.

"Let's get some shit straight. First off, hoe, my girl ain't the bitch, you are. Second, if you try to start any trouble with my wifey in my establishment, we will have serious problems. So, I advise you to sit back, enjoy the muthafuckin' night, and pretend you don't know me. Clear?"

"Yaseer, I don't give a flying fuck about that hoe you got tagging along with you tonight. Fuck ha! Nigga, you wasn't worried about her when you was all up in this pussy! Matter of fact, I think it's time she found out. What you think?" Ariel asked with a smirk.

Yaseer took his hand and grabbed her by her throat, squeezing tightly and almost cutting off her circulation. Then he bent down close to her ear and said, "Fuck with me if you want to, bitch, and yo ass will end up being my pit bull's next meal. I will toe tag yo ass and then sleep peacefully without losing a wink of sleep. I could give two shits about yo whoring ass. You knew I had a girl when you started fuckin' with me, so don't act brand new. You was a good fuck, bitch, and that's all you will ever be. As a matter of fact, get out my club before I outline yo ass in chalk," Yaseer stated as he let her go. Then he walked off to handle his business in the bathroom.

Ariel wanted to cry because her feelings were hurt, but at the same time she was turned on. She liked when he got rough with her, but the hurtful words such as calling her hoes and shit, she could do without.

After emptying his bladder, Yaseer walked back to where his crew was chilling with bottles of Rosé, Patron, and Cîroc, ignoring Ariel on the way to his seat. He sat down next to his reason for existing.

"Now why you embarrass that girl like that?" Paris asked laughing.

"Sheeiitt, had your ass heard what she said, I would be pulling you off of her." He paused to take a sip of his Rosé then stood up, grabbed Paris' hand and pulled her up at the same time. "Come on bae, let's go dance. This is our song they playing." He gently tugged at her hand and she followed him to the dance floor.

Once they were in his desired spot, he pulled her close to him and started moving to the beat of the music. Jagged Edge's song *Promise* blasted through the speakers. He held her closely and sang the old-school lyrics in her ear.

"Nothin' is promised, to me and you/ So why will we let this thing go?/ Baby I promise, that I'll stay true/ Don't let nobody say it ain't so/ Baby I promise that I'll never leave/ And everything will be alright, I/ I promise, these things to you/ Girl just believe/ I promise."

Paris loved to hear him sing to her because he could actually carry a tune. They continued to sway to the music as it flowed to more up-to-date music. The lyrics to Sevyn Streeter's *It Won't Stop* was booming through the speakers and had them in their own little world.

"With every single part of me/ My love for you is constantly/ Forever and ever on repeat, on repeat (oh)/ And it won't stop/ Oh oh oh oh oh oh/ Every day, every day/ I can't breathe/ You take my breath away from me/ Here's my heart/ You got the key/ Put that on eternity/ I love you 'til infinity."

Yaseer looked down at the beautiful woman he held in his embrace. His heart filled with so much love for her it felt like it was about to explode.

"You know I love you. There ain't one piece of pussy that can change that shit. You got my heart. You're the reason why I hustle so hard. I don't know what I did to deserve so much of your heart, but what I do know is, I love you more than I love myself. As soon as we can, we are getting out of this and goin' all the way legit. Just continue to hang with me, gorgeous," Yaseer said to Paris, getting a little emotional in the process. Then he lifted his hand to signal the deejay to stop the music.

Paris looked at Yaseer through misty eyes. Before she could even respond, he was on bended knee with a six carat princess cut engagement ring between his thumb and index finger.

"Before everyone here, I want to declare my love for you by asking you to be my wife. Paris Alexandria Jacobs, Will you mar—"

"Yes! Yes! Yes!" Paris screamed impatiently before he could finish the question.

He placed the ring on her finger and stood to hug and kiss her. She had just made him the happiest man in the world. The crowd erupted with applause and plenty of congratulations. They partied for a little while longer before Yaseer told the crew that he and Paris were about to dip.

As they walked outside to go get in the car, shots erupted out of nowhere sending bullets flying in their direction. Yaseer went for his piece and started busting at the fools who were aiming for them from across the parking lot. He tried to shield Paris, but she moved from behind him and was poppin' off her twin Nines he had bought for her.

"Shit," he yelled after a bullet grazed his left arm.

Paris hit two targets in the head, killing them instantly. Yaseer hit two other men, one in the chest and the second in the eye through the head, killing them as well. Finally, he shot the last dude, but left him alive to be questioned before he dismantled his body. Evidently, someone had seen what was about to go down because his crew came running out with their tools in hand, ready to bust.

Yaseer walked over to the last breathing gunman with his crew on his heels. As soon as he got over to him, he lifted his size thirteen and started stomping the bastard until he felt good and

---

---

tired. He was on pure adrenalin and as of that moment, he wasn't feeling shit but anger.

"Grab this fool and meet me at The Chambers," he said to his crew before motioning with his hand for Paris to come on. His adrenalin high was starting to wear off. He was beginning to feel the pain in his arm, and it felt like it was on fire.

Yaseer handed the keys to Paris. There was no way he could drive. She started up the car, put it in gear, and sped out of the parking lot like she was damn near on the *Fast and Furious* movie. She checked the rearview mirror and saw the crew pushing their whips beside and behind her.

Ezra called Yaseer fuming. "Yo bruh, what the fuck going on?"

"Fuck if I know! Just get that fool to The Chambers now! We will meet you there," Yaseer responded angrily.

*****

25

Paris parked the car, and popped the trunk as they were getting out.

His blood was boiling just thinking about the shit that had just gone down. He peered down into the trunk and felt like murking that nigga right then and there. But he knew they needed answers, so he checked his feelings as best as he could so he could handle business.

Yaseer and Paris walked over to Kai'yan's car where the victim was.

"Yo, Lee, help me get this obituary out my damn trunk," Yan said, referring to the soon to be dead man.

"A'ight," was Liam's response.

Liam grabbed his legs while Kai'yan grabbed their victim's arms. Brooklyn walked over to them so she could shut Yan's trunk while the two men carried their attacker inside with Ezra, Brooklyn, and London on their heels. They took him into the waiting room of the first office and strapped him to one of the chairs they had specially made for moments such as these. The chair had restraints all around it to make sure whoever was strapped in could not move. The restraints were impossible to get out of. Shit was about to get dumb wild.

Chapter 3

Zuri slowly opened his eyes. Everything seemed so fuzzy. He felt like he had been asleep for about a decade. He had lost a lot of blood from his bullet wound. As he came to, he noticed people standing around looking at him with their arms folded across their chest. In the center, stood Yaseer.

"Oh, shit," was all he could think. Zuri knew how they got down. Hell, he had seen Yaseer in action when he used a blow torch and alcohol to burn a guy they knew from around the way piece by piece.

Zuri was accustomed to the Helen Keller street code of conduct. You ain't hear nothing, you ain't seen nothing. That night he just so happened to be at the wrong place, wrong time and with the wrong person. After that night, he stayed out of Yaseer's way, but just that one night put him on his radar and that is exactly why Yaseer knew who he and his family was. Zuri knew this was the end. His fate was sealed.

Zuri was scared as fuck, but he wasn't about to let them know that. And he damn sure wasn't about to go out like a pussy. He didn't have a big ass letter G tatted across his heart for nothing. He came out a woman's pussy into this world as a G and was going to be put in the dirt as one.

"What's up muthafucka? Time to wakey-wakey and get this show on the road," Yaseer said smirking.

"Fuck is you, pussy nigga?" Zuri said with a hint of attitude.

"Ooohhh, snap. He wake up talking shit. I guess him a widdle upset," London said with her bottom lip poked out before she started laughing.

Zuri was piping hot. He couldn't stand a bitch that didn't know how to shut up, especially one with a smart mouth.

"Look, you fuckin' up my night. My fiancé's pussy is hot, wet, and waiting on me to go in balls deep, so please don't waste my time. You see that huge circular medal tub over there?" Yaseer asked him.

"Yea, and?"

"It's filled with boiling hot grease. If by the third time I ask you my question, you still haven't answered it or told me what I want to hear, I'ma drop your ass in that tub and fry you like a piece of Kentucky fried chicken. Then I'm going to chop you up into bite-size nugget pieces, portion them out, box them up, and have them to delivered to your family members, including yo baby momma and son that stay over there on the east side of Charlotte. Now, if you tell me what I want to hear, then I will make it easy and just chop your head off. It's up to you. So with that being said, who sent you after me?" Yaseer questioned.

"Yo momma did, bitch!"

Yaseer backhanded the shit out of him. Zuri felt his lip start to swell.

"Who sent you after me and mines?" he asked again.

"That pretty little pussy beside you did!"

Zuri said, looking at Paris.

Paris walked over to him, got eye to eye level with him and said in a sultry voice, "Thanks for the compliment baby, but that lie is 'bout to cost ya." She immediately took a blade and sliced his face from his side burns to his lying lips. Standing back, she smirked in admiration of her work before walking back over to stand beside her man.

Zuri yelped. He was starting to feel a little dizzy and wanted them to hurry up and kill him. But he refused to be a snitch, so he would take this shit like a man.

"This ya last chance to answer me. Now who sent you?" Yaseer asked one final time. He was irritated as fuck because he was in pain and dude was choosing the wrong time to get his comedy central on instead of answering his question.

"That bitch over there," Zuri said, looking at Brooklyn.

Brook pulled out her Glock .50 and shot him

right between the legs, sending blood and ball juice flying. Since he wanted to be a pussy, she decided to help him achieve his goal.

"Aaahhhh, fuck!" Zuri screamed with tears streaming down from his eyes.

"I guess thugs do cry," Brooklyn said as she shrugged her shoulders and popped a piece of gum in her mouth like she didn't have a care in the world.

"Hope ya son's favorite food is nuggets!" Yaseer stated as he unstrapped Zuri from the chair, picked him up by the throat with the hand on his good arm, and walked over to the tub of hot grease with the pathetic joke of a gangster.

Zuri used his hands to try to remove the vice grip Yaseer's hand had around his neck. But Yaseer lifted Zuri's small frame up and dropped him in the piping hot grease. The grease started popping extremely loud as he screamed for dear life. But it wasn't long before he took his last breath.

"Ezra, come stitch this graze up for me,"

Yaseer instructed.

Ezra had a little medical training. He had graduated from medical school, but the medical field wasn't for him. He'd only gone to have something to do. Ezra was stupid intelligent, like *hack CIA shit and get away with it* smart. So, he had a few degrees under his belt at the age of twenty six.

"A'ight, let me grab my tools Yas, then I got you," he replied.

Yaseer was a man of his word so the next day, as promised, he had Zuri's body parts cut up, placed in small boxes like Chick-Fil-A nuggets, and delivered to all of his family, saving Zuri's baby moms and seed for last.

After Yaseer got done delivering Zuri to his family, he started making his way over to his brother's house. He pulled up to Liam's crib, turned his car off and just sat for a minute, thinking. He had no clue who was aiming at him. Being in the game, he knew that haters were constant. But damn, the majority of the time he knew who the hatin' fuckas were. Somebody was gonna tell him something and he didn't give a fuck who he had to go through or kill to get the answers. Niggas had the game twisted. He ran shit.

Yaseer leaned his head back on his headrest and wondered who was testing their luck. The last time a fool tried him, the dude never took another breath again. He remembered one time a guy he knew from across the way named Xavier tried to jump MJ to get back at him. Xavier was mad because Yaseer wouldn't come down on his prices since he was already giving him a deal on the bricks. He was being more than fair. There was no way in hell he was about to lower his prices any more.

Yaseer recalled that day clearly. The muthafucka wanted to be a Billy Bad Ass.

"Fuck you and your product nigga! I ain't paying that shit, matter of fact, you 'bout to come up off all that for free ninety-nine plus tax!" Then

he rose up like he was about to try something.

Wrong move. Yaseer yanked out his .45 and shot the bastard twice, once in both knees.

"Bitch nigga, you think you hard, huh!? Your dumb ass shoulda took the deal I offered. Now I'm 'bout to get myself a sweet deal. I'm 'bout to take your money and your life! Now tax that, pussy nigga," Yaseer yelled. He looked to his left and told Yan to take the idiot to room three.

"Which method we using tonight?" Yan asked him.

"Melt down since he wanted to act like a bitch and have one," Yaseer replied with a sneer.

Yan took Xavier to The Chamber and strapped him to a chair. It was about to get crazy in two point nine seconds.

"You better hope you kill me 'cause I promise I'ma lay ya whole squad out if you don't,"

Xavier yelled in a frustrated voice.

"Oh, don't worry, we will," Yan replied. "Aye, Ezra, hand me the machetes, get the chains,

and fill a bucket with acid," Yaseer heard Yan say as he walked in moments later.

"Everything's set up?" Yaseer asked Yan and Ezra.

"Yea, Boss, we already ready," was their response to him.

He walked over to a pissed off Xavier and smacked him with the butt of his gun. Blood along with a tooth, flew out of Xavier's mouth. But surprisingly, all he did was wince.

Yaseer knew from growing up with him that he wasn't a punk, but the bastard was stupid and a hot head, which was the reason his stupid, hot-headed ass was about to lose his life.

"Hand me the chains," Yaseer ordered.

Yan handed him the chains. He took the chains and wrapped them around his hands like a black momma did a belt when she was about to whoop her Bébé kid's ass, stepped back, lifted the chain in his hand, and swung as hard as he could, hitting Xavier across the chest. When he heard his collarbone crack, Yaseer knew that he had broken it.

"Shit," Xavier growled out through clenched teeth.

"Nah, muthafucka, you hard. Don't start moaning and groaning like a bitch now," Yaseer said to him.

"Fuck you!" Xavier responded. That only egged Yaseer on more.

"Yea, yea, it's always fuck you, you better kill me, bitch nigga this and bitch nigga that, please don't kill me, I'm sorry— Yada, yada, yada. The end result is all that matters," Yaseer replied, hitting Xavier two more times with the chain.

This time it went skin deep, sending blood everywhere on the second hit. Now the nigga was literally crying. He should have known not to try and bitch Yaseer down. He didn't play that shit with no fuckin' one.

"Go get the acid, Ezra," Yaseer demanded.

When Ezra walked back in with a bucket

acid, Yaseer said, "A'ight nigga, it's time to burn some skin cells." He then took both of Xavier's hands and put them in the acid. Xavier screamed for dear life as his skin melted off of his fingers like candle wax.

"Thanks, my brutha. It was very thoughtful of you to loan me your unwanted skin," Yaseer said with a huge ass grin on his face. After that, he pulled on his black leather gloves, grabbed his machete, and cut Xavier's head off.

"Get this trash out of my building," he said to Ezra as he patted him on the back and left out.

So needless to say, nobody fucked with Yaseer. Better yet, no one fucked around with his team on some hating shit unless they were on a suicide mission.

So why in the fuck fools wanted to test his gangster like he was getting soft, he had no clue. But evidently, the nigga had a death wish. And what kind of person would he be if he didn't appease his enemy's last wishes? He shook his head at how wild things were about to become. These fool's didn't know what trouble they had awoken, but they were sure in the hell about to find out.

Chapter 4

Yaseer got out of the car and walked up to the door, preparing to use the key that Liam had given him. But as soon as he was about to insert his key into the lock, the door opened. Liam had seen him approaching the door on the cameras he had set up outside. Every member of their team had cameras on their homes as a safety precaution. Yaseer walked in and dapped up Kai'yan as he closed the door behind himself.

"Sup, boy, what's poppin' with ya?" Yaseer asked.

"Ain't shit, just keeping my ears to the street you know how I do. Where wifey at?" Kai'yan responded.

"Yea, you know I know how ya get down, my ninja, and she at home. London was just getting their when I left. Set the card table up, we gon' sit here and try to piece this shit together over a game. You know I think better when my mind is more relaxed. Let me grab a beer right quick before I come down stairs though," Yaseer replied.

"A'ight, bruh," was Yan's response. Yaseer had known Kai'yan most of his teenage life up until now. He and Yan had grown up on the streets together. After Yaseer's parents got knocked by the jakes for drug distribution, he was determined to get money. He refused to allow his siblings or him to be hungry. His parents had money stashed away for them. But he knew that it was bound to run out sooner or later, so he started hustling.

During that time is when he met Kai'yan. Their backgrounds were similar, except Kai'yan's parents were killed by a Judas nigga who was breaking bread with the enemy while plotting their demise. Once the nigga got his Wheaties up, the motherfucker decided to act on his ill feelings. Needless to say, he succeeded due to the fact that Yan's parents never suspected any foul play from the guy because he was like family. It was a very dumb move on the killer's behalf to let Kai'yan live because no less than a year later Yan tracked him down and shot him right in the middle of his head in front of his woman.

Yaseer loved Kai'yan like a blood brother. Blood couldn't make them any closer than they already were. He knew Yan would murk a fool on sight for him and vice versa. He was about to head downstairs to the man cave that Liam had set up when the doorbell rang. He turned around to go answer the door. Once he got to the door, he looked out of the peep hole to see who it was. It was his boy, Ezra.

"Wus good, son?" Yaseer said, dapping him up after opening the door.

"Ain't shit, fuck ya clowns up to?" Ezra responded.

"Not a damn thing. 'Bout to whoop some ass on the table."

"You already know I'm 'bout to take all y'all paper so you might as well just hand it over now."

"Sshheeiittt, not with me and Yan you not, you know between me and him we stay taking a muthafucka bread," Yaseer replied laughing.

"Stop playing! You know I'm the king in this shit," Ezra said.

"Fuck outta here with that, son! You already know you can't see me on that table, bruh."

"Wanna bet a G that I'ma spank that ass?" was Ezra's response.

"Sheeiitt, you ain't said nothin' but a word, home skillet biscuit," Yaseer said, ready to take his boy's stripper money.

"A'ight, don't get muhfuckin' amnesia when it's time to hand them winnings over," Ezra said.

"Oh, I pays my debts, believe that," Yaseer responded. He and Ezra were almost to the bottom step when they heard Liam start talking junk.

"Fuck y'all was up their doing, singing *Kumbaya* or sumthin'? Bring y'all asses on."

They entered what had been deemed their man cave. The shit was ridonkulous how they had set it up. They had the room painted black and accented with gold. The black carpet in that joint was stupid soft. It was that fluffy type of carpet. Then they had photos of famous black people like Michael Jackson, Maya Angelou, Paul Laurence Dunbar, Michael Jordan, Jackie Robinson, Rosa Parks, MLK, Mike Tyson, Malcolm X and Obama. And that was only a handful of the pictures that laced the walls in the cave. No matter how rich they became, none of them ever forgot their heritage or how far African Americans have come.

They also had the room decked out with a 70" plasma TV, complete with game systems such as a PS4, XBOX 360, Wii etc. Surround sound speakers hung in the corners of the room. On top of that, they had a mini bar, a pool table, a hockey table, and last but not least, the card table where they sat when they needed to clear their heads or figure shit out. Somehow, that's how they figured out a lot of things.

"Nigga, we was coming. Get ya thong out

cha asshole," Yaseer responded.

"Fuck you, nigga," Liam said, cracking a smile.

"Fuck me?" Yaseer asked as he placed his hand on his chest putting on his best performance pretending like his feelings were hurt before continuing on with his comment. "No, no nigga, fuck you and the bullshit you shittin' out your mouth, too," he said, cracking up at his own joke.

The crew burst out laughing, too. This was the only time things were not so stressful. Yaseer knew they had to get serious in a few. But at that very moment, he needed a good laugh.

"Smart ass!" Liam replied.

By the third game, Yaseer's income had increased by an extra three bands, plus a stack Ezra owed him. Yaseer placed his cards on the table so he could start discussing the situation at hand.

"Listen up, them cats who came bussin' at me and mines just didn't wake up one minute and say, 'Let's go play Russian Roulette with our lives today.' Someone had sent them to take wifey and me out. Now we got to figure out who sent them. Has anyone heard anything on the streets about who sent those non-shooting pricks my way?" Yaseer asked no one in particular.

"Yas, I'ma be honest wit ya, bruh. Everybody I'm questioning about it acting like they shook and shit. I don't know who aiming this way but muhfuckas ain't tryna speak on whoever it is. We really gonna have to comb the streets thoroughly. I know someone know something," Ezra answered.

Everyone else pretty much said the same thing Ezra had.

"I tell you what I know. Crack heads will do anything for half a brick. So, this is what we going to do. We 'bout to put up a reward for six G's and a half a brick for whoever gives us any info they may have. And if they lead the fool to us, they get the other half of the brick," Yaseer said.

One thing he knew was that junkies would

give up their own moms and kids to chase that high. If no one gave up answers after that was put out there, then he was going to sit down and re-evaluate shit because he knew the fool had to have been politicking with some idiot or Judas nigga about his plans.

After a few more rounds of cards, Yaseer stood and started saying his goodbyes so he could start trying to piece things together by himself.

"I'ma fuck with y'all later on. Let me go home to feed and walk Diamond and Princeton. Y'all know Paris ass ain't fuckin with them dogs."

"You and them damn bitches." Ezra said with a voice full of laughter.

"And you the biggest bitch of them all." Yaseer cracked back, garnishing a laugh from everyone except Ezra. He just smirked at the comment knowing he didn't have a comeback to top that.

"I'm out y'all." Yaseer said, dapping everyone up before turning to leave.

47

Chapter 5

"A'ight, bruh. I'ma get ya later 'bout some shit. Be cool," Yaseer said to Kai'yan as he walked with him to the door to lock it.

"Aye, Yas, let me put some hot shit in ya ear right quick," Kai'yan said once they got to the door.

Yaseer motioned for him to follow him outside. He knew it was something serious because that's pretty much the only time Yan used that line.

"Let's sit in my car. It's cold as fuck out here, bruh," Yaseer said while walking to his Bentley. He unlocked the car and slid in. Kai'yan followed suit.

"What's on ya mind, son?" Yaseer asked, looking at Kai'yan.

"I'ma get straight to the point, bruh. I need you to watch who you calling family, my nigga, 'cause everything ain't as it appears and everything that glitters ain't gold. I been questioning and shit not adding up. I don't know who aiming for you exactly, but I got a feeling its closer to home than what we think. Be careful Yas, and please watch ya back with everyone, family too. That's all I wanted to tell you, son," Kai'yan said, and then opened the door to get out.

Yaseer grabbed his arm to stop him. "How strong is this feeling you been having?" Yaseer asked him.

"Stronger than the force of a speeding train hitting a car that's stuck on its tracks," he replied before getting out and going back inside.

Yaseer took his words very seriously. When Kai'yan got feelings like those, Yaseer barely ignored them because the majority of the time it was those feelings that kept them alive when they were hustling on the streets. He needed answers and he needed them now. When niggas wanted you out of the way, they didn't stop until they achieved that goal and he refused to let his crew or his life be snuffed out by the enemy.

Yaseer pulled away from his brother's house with a lot on his brain. Finding a way to trap his unknown enemy was his front and center thought.

*****

Paris sat on the bed with a pillow propped in between her back and the headboard, reading *Thugs Cry 2* by her favorite author, Ca$h, waiting for Yaseer to come home.

She had just gotten to the part in the story were Raheem was hugging his boy, begging him to hold on to life after getting shot when she heard Yaseer enter the house.

Paris popped up off the bed like a jack in the box. She had been waiting all day for him, reading about these niggas had her dripping wet for her own man. Paris raced downstairs to meet him.

"Hey, babe!" she exclaimed, excitedly reaching out to hug him.

"Hey, baby love. What you been up to all day?" Yaseer inquired as he pulled her close to him and palmed her protruding behind.

"Nothing much, reading and thinking about you."

"A'ight, nah, don't make me shoot them niggas up in that book you reading. They getting more face time than me."

Paris burst out laughing. "Let me find out you jelly about fictional characters."

"Hell yea!" Yaseer spat with a smirk on his face.

Paris stood on her tippy toes and kissed Yaseer slowly and deliberately.

"Can the men in that book feel that? Or this?" Paris seductively asked, cupping Yaseer's member in her hand through his jeans.

Yaseer's dick grew harder than concrete.

"I don't know, bae, they might. Go a little further so I can make sure they not feeling what I'm feeling or about to get right now," Yaseer answered, hoping she would do the thing he loved most, which was give him some face.

His prayer was answered when Paris lowered her body in front of him, unbuttoned and unzipped his pants, then proceeded to pull his steel out of its cage and place it between her wet juicy lips.

Paris took the tip of her tongue and licked the vein on the underside of his penis before sucking it in between her wet juicy lips. Paris went to work sucking on him like a person who had been deprived meat all their life and was just now getting their first taste.

Paris pulled back and spat on Yaseer's dick then began to pump her hand up and down on it. Paris kept using her hand to pump him as she brought her tongue out to show Yaseer's family jewels some appreciation as well. She suctioned them in her lips one by one being sure to show them both equal appreciation, then she proceeded to lick her way up his swollen penis swirling her tongue along the way before pulling it back into her mouth and deep throating him.

Yaseer was on the verge of shooting off early, and that was something he was not ready to do.

"Ba- baaee, hho-hhole up," Yaseer moaned out trying to capture Paris' attention.

Paris kept slurping like she was trying to win the dick-sucking award of the year, ignoring Yaseer's pleas. He felt himself about to shoot off. He pulled away from her mouth, bent over and scooped her into his arms, carrying her upstairs, dick swinging and all.

Once Yaseer got inside of their room, he laid Paris on their California King and then pulled her bottom to the edge of the bed. He hooked his fingers in the band of the tiny black boy shorts she had on and pulled them down her thick thighs. It was his turn to return the favor.

Yaseer bent down close to her honey spot and let his tongue out to play in its favorite playground. Her soft moans approached his ears like a classical piece of music being played.

He leaned up to admire the lower half of her body then decided he needed to see more. So he reached under the hem of her baby tee to discard the garment. He wanted her fully naked so that when she reached her peak and her back arched up off of the bed in that beautiful arch that he loved to see, he could admire her body in its natural form. Each time she was unclothed before him, she left him breathless. It was just something about her beauty. It struck him each and every time as if he was seeing it for the first time.

With her pecan tan twin globes peering out at him, Yaseer worked his way back down her body and in between her legs. Eye to eye with his meal, ready to thoroughly enjoy his feast, he leaned forward and stuck his tongue out to taste her sweet nectar. He could hear her moaning out his name. He didn't plan to rush. He planned to take his sweet time making love to the other half of him. Her hands clutched the bed spread as he used his tongue going in and out of her feminine tunnel in the same rhythm he planned to mimic with his dick in a few. He continued licking her succulent lower lips and tantalizing her pearl.

She cried out, "Bae, I need to feel you deep inside of me. I can't wait any longer."

Yaseer was as hard as stone. He stood up, guided his manhood inside of Paris until he was buried to the hilt. Yaseer let an explicative word pass through his lips as he began to pump in and out of her in a fluid motion.

He took her right leg and placed it in between the crook of his arm so he could hit the spot inside of her he knew would drive her insane. He was aiming for her G spot and with very little effort he was able to find it.

Once he found that spot he grinded into it with slow pumps going deep then pulling back like he planned to exit only to plunge back in.

"Oh, shit. Harder, Yaseer. Harder," Paris moaned. She pulled him in deeper.

Yaseer put her legs on his shoulders so he

could go deeper. It was pure ecstasy. He began to pound her inside like a bass drum. He relished in the sounds of his balls slapping up against her ass.

Paris' nails dug deep into his back as she moaned out his name over and over.

"Fuck!" Yaseer growled through clenched teeth when Paris' vagina started contracting around his dick. His load shot through her with such an intensity that it made her explode again just from the feeling.

They stayed up practically the whole night, taking turns pleasing one another's body.

The next morning, Paris was awakened to the smell of breakfast being cooked. Her stomach growled, notifying her that it was ready to be fed.

She threw her shapely legs over the edge of the bed and just sat there for a brief moment, thanking the good Lord above for blessing her with such a good man.

Paris stood up, fully nude, and made her

way down stairs in search for her man. She found him standing over the stove shirtless with his black, red, and white basketball shorts on.

Yaseer turned halfway around, revealing his caramel six-pack, and blessed Paris with a beautiful smile before he spoke.

"Hey, bae, I didn't want to wake you but I figured you would be hungry by the time you got up, so I decided to fix you breakfast before I got ready to go take care of some business."

"Aww, look at my man tryna be sweet," Paris said with a smirk as she made her way over to where Yaseer stood.

"You got jokes. You know your ass is more rotten than some week old chitlins," Yaseer replied and then smacked Paris on her butt on his way to get some juice out of the refrigerator. He took out some Minute Maid Berry Punch and poured some in a glass for himself and Paris. Then he placed the box of juice back in the refrigerator.

"Don't I know it," Paris responded with a

giggle.

Yaseer fixed his and Paris' plates. Paris eyed the food with wide eyes. All the love-making they had done the night before and that morning had her starved.

He had fixed pancakes, grits, eggs, turkey sausage, and fruit salad. Paris picked up her fork and dove straight in. After they completed their meals, they went upstairs, showered, dressed, and got prepared for what the day might hold for them.

"Babe, can you drop me off at London's?" Paris asked as they descended the staircase.

"Yea, what y'all got planned for today?

"Nothing much, just going out to eat and to the movies. That's about it."

"That's what's up. Hold up right quick." Yaseer stopped in front of the door, reached in his pocket, and pulled out his wallet. He handed her his Visa Black card. "Make sure you get something that will make my dick jump when I see it on you later on tonight."

Paris couldn't help but smile. Her man was the truth and she knew it. Her panties got soaked thinking about what was to come later on that night. And with that thought, she followed Yaseer out of the door to the car, thinking of a way to seduce her man that night.

Chapter 6

Yaseer watched to make sure Paris made it into London's house okay before pulling out of the driveway and heading in the direction of Harris Blvd. off Albemarle Rd. to holler at his mans, Money D.

Yaseer pulled into Sandlewood Apartments. Everyone that lived there or grew up around there called the complex Sandlehood Apartments because of all the crime that happened there. Yaseer was beyond happy that he didn't have to stay in them anymore. He spotted his boy standing in front of his apartment at the bottom of the stairwell.

Yaseer parked his car and hopped out looking fresh as fuck, rockin' a crisp royal blue T-shirt, some black Robin jeans, and a pair of twenty-threes with a black NY fitted, and his TTC chain. He was on point. He nodded at some hoes that sat in a stairwell across from D smoking some weed. A bad red-bone sat in the middle of them along with a beautiful chocolate sista, but they were straight jailbait so he kept on stepping. His girl and his side pussy was enough for him. But every now and then when he saw a dime brizzle, he would look. D met him halfway.

"What's good wit cha?" D said while dapping him up.

"Sheeiit, can't call it. Nigga, yo ass stay in muthafuckin' wife beaters and black basketball shorts with fuckin' J's. I swear you done claimed every pair of black and red Jordan's that was ever invented," Yaseer said to him.

"That's the only way to go. Red and black all day," was D's response.

"On a serious note, I came to politic with ya for a quick sec," Yaseer said as he followed D into his apartment.

D was a little brown skin nigga, but as small as he was, he had serious heart and he ain't never had no problem pulling that tool on a fool who wanted it. The majority of the time, niggas knew not to mess with him. However, the females loved him. They stayed flocking to him. He had dang near ten kids.

Yaseer dealt with D and his homeboy, Krome, the long way because he knew neither one would screw him over. They were both one hundred percent thoroughbred niggas, hence the reason he was there. He needed to see if D had heard anything in the streets about what had gone down at his club. He needed some info about this more than a single momma on welfare needed her check on the first of the month, and hopefully his boy could help him out.

"So, wus poppin' wit cha my G?" D asked him while grabbing a seat.

"A'ight, bruh, I know you heard about me and my lady gettin' attacked and shit."

D nodded his head up and down. "Yea, I did. I'm sorry to hear that shit happened, bruh. That was some fucked up shit," he said, looking at

Yaseer with genuine concern laced on his face.

"Yea, man, that shit fuckin' with a G real bad, especially since I don't have a clue who behind the shit. Have you heard anything on the streets?" Yaseer responded.

"Nah, not that I can think of. You want me to have Krome put his ear to the street? You already know I'm ready to pop a muthafucka," D replied.

"Yea, tell 'em to listen out for me. And I know yo trigga happy ass ready to shoot sum'n."

They both had to laugh at Yaseer's accurate comment because they both knew the truth was all up and through that statement.

"Where ya shorty at?" Yaseer asked.

"She over her mom's crib with the kids and shit. You know how that go."

"Hell yea, what yo ass got about thirteen kids now?" Yaseer clowned with a slight chuckle.

"Man, fuck you! Your corny ass got jokey jokes. Nah muhfucka, you know I only got six. Stop playin', son," D responded, laughing as well. "How da fuck yo ass forget how many seeds I got when you they damn God Daddy? Fuck outta here," D said, laughing at his boy.

"Well shit, the way yo ass poppin' up with all these damn kids everywhere, ain't no way I can keep up. Every time I turn around you got another female pregnant. Nigga, yo ass ain't nun but twenty four and you already at six. Damn my G, your ass need to get fuckin' snipped!" Yaseer spat.

"I wish the fuck I would! I just had a lil' shorty I been fuckin' wit call me last night talkin' bout she pregnant. Now I gotta explain this shit to fuckin' Krista," D said without a care in the world.

"See what I mean. Nigga wrap yo shit up. Yo ass bring something home, Krista gone kill yo ass. Keep fuckin' 'round if you want to," Yaseer warned.

"How yo ass gon' talk shit when you be slinging the D more than me?"

"'Cause I only go raw dog in one pussy, that's how," Yaseer answered.

"I feel ya," D responded.

They sat and chopped it up for a little while longer until it was time for Yaseer to bounce. He had to go get Paris from the mall.

*****

"I can't believe this shit," London said to Brooklyn while they stood by the bathroom door waiting on Paris to come out.

"Me either, girl. I can't wait 'til we find the bastard who even thought to try and touch my blood, let alone my future sister-in-law. That was some real fuck shit. I know somebody know something," Brooklyn said to London.

The girls had decided to go do a little retail therapy at Northlake Mall and grab a bite to eat.

"Well, I'm pretty sure someone gon' dig up the info soon. Ain't no way Yas 'bout to let shit ride. His ass plays no games. Anyways, how shit flowing between you and Kai'yan? I assume Yaseer still out of the loop about you two," London said to

Brooklyn.

"Everything is going well between us. He has been begging me to go to Yaseer to tell him we are together. You know he likes to keep shit a thousand with Yaseer. But I'm just not ready to deal with Yas or Liam's overprotective asses yet. Plus, with all this shit going on, it's the wrong time to bring it up," Brooklyn responded.

"I feel ya," was London's response.

"What I miss?" Paris asked while exiting the bathroom.

"Not a damn thing Nosetta Stone," London replied.

"Smart ass! So sis, what's going on between you and Liam?" Paris asked London as they began walking to the food court.

"Not a damn thing! That nigga flirt with anything that has titties and a hole between their thighs. He wish he could get a piece of this good-good. I ain't gonna lie though, that brown nigga fine as hell, the way his swag is, and the way his

67

chiseled 6'1" frame is built… sshhheeiiitt be having a bitch ready to drop her drawers when he open his mouth and talk with that deep voice and up north accent. But like I said, ain't nothin' goin' on between me and his sexy ass," London concluded her answer.

"Who the hell answers a question like that? Bitch, how ya ass gon' say ain't nothing going on between y'all but sit there and get all drippy wet talking about his voice and shit. You a damn mess, you know that right? I swear yo ass ride the short yella bus," Paris responded while giving London the side eye. Then she had to laugh at her sister's shenanigans.

London's ass was crazy but she loved her and wouldn't have her any other way.

"Bitch, yo ass was sitting right next to me with a helmet on, too, don't front!" London said cracking up.

"In the words of my boy Chris Tucker, *'And you know this maann,'*" Paris replied, laughing, too.

Brooklyn shook her head at them and had to laugh as well. Seeing those two go back and forth was hilarious.

After the chuckling died down, things turned serious.

"Y'all we got to be careful. You know when niggas trying to take a nigga's throne, they will do anything to get it, even harm a niggas loved ones. That's the way the game goes," London said to both Paris and Brooklyn.

Brook and Paris both nodded their heads, thinking of just how serious this situation was. They could all handle themselves. It was just the fear of the unknown that was the problem. It's a whole new ball game when niggas start popping out of nowhere like a fucking Jack-in-the-box. The girls finished their meal, got up, and threw away their trash. Then they continued shopping until Yaseer got there to pick up Paris.

Chapter 7

Yaseer pulled up to the mall entrance around 8:30PM and waited for his lady to come out. He texted her to let her know he was outside. It had been a long day and he was ready to go home and chill out for the night.

His girl walked out looking sexy as hell in her Balmain jeans and royal purple cameo with a black blazer over it. He got out of the car to open the door for her and help her with her bags.

Paris looked like she had bought the whole damn mall, but Yaseer didn't care. They had money out of the butt and she deserved any little thing her beautiful heart desired. He helped her into the car, then went to get back in the driver's seat and pulled off.

"Did you enjoy yourself?" Yaseer asked.

"Yea, how could I not enjoy myself around your sister and London's cray-cray self?" she responded.

"That's good. I'm glad you enjoyed yourself, sweetie. What you tryna do the rest of the day, bae?"

"You," was her response.

"A'ight, don't start shit that your ass can't finish. You know as soon as I hit that spot yo ass be tryna run from the dick," Yaseer replied, looking over at her, smirking.

Paris didn't even bother to respond verbally. Instead, she took her hand and eased it over the zipper of his jeans and slid it down. She eased her hand inside of them and pulled Yaseer's steel out.

Oh, shit, Yaseer swore to himself. He knew just what she was about to do. *Damn, now why my ass had to say something slick, knowing how my baby do?* Yaseer thought to himself.

Paris undid her seat belt, leaned over and eased the head of his dick into her mouth. Then she pulled back and took the tip of her tongue and swirled it around the top, and then up and down the vain on the underside of his dick. Yaseer was as hard as stone. He almost crashed into the car in front of him when she took all of him in her mouth and began deep throating him.

"Paris-ba-bae wwaai-wait til we get home," he stuttered. He was about to erupt in point two seconds if she didn't stop.

Yaseer pulled over to the shoulder of the road because Paris' crazy self would mess around and get them pulled over because of her head game. He turned on his hazard lights and put the car into park. He leaned his head back for what seemed like a brief second. Before he knew it, his body started to spasm as if he had been struck by lightning. His seeds shot down her throat. He didn't even try to pull her back.

Paris drunk his cum like she was dying of thirst and then sat up, licked her lips, smiled at him, and actually had the nerve to ask Yaseer why he had pulled over.

Yaseer had something for her, though. They had barely got in the house good when Yaseer pulled Paris' arm and spun her around to face him. "So you thought you was funny, right?" Yaseer whispered in her ear as he pushed her backwards against the door with his body.

Paris responded with silence. She knew she was in trouble but she wasn't worried, she was about to enjoy her punishment immensely.

"Don't get quiet on me now, shorty." Yaseer whispered close to her lips as his hand slid down the waistband of her pants and panties. He caressed the moist folds of her flesh before he inserted his middle finger deep inside of Paris' punani.

Paris gasped deeply and held her breath for a split second. Yaseer leaned forward and began placing kisses on the side of her neck using his tongue to tease her hot spot right below her ear before pulling her skin into his mouth and sucking on it making sure to leave his mark.

Yaseer lifted his head ever so slightly to look at the expression on Paris' face. He loved to see her in this blissful state and he wanted to be in that same place right along with her.

Without a word Yaseer smoothly unbuttoned her pants with his free hand, then yanked them down causing Paris to open her eyes halfway to look at him. Yaseer undid his pants and let his jeans fall down to his ankles. Using his knee, he parted Paris' legs wider for easier access, then slid inside of her pussy hard and deep.

Yaseer gritted his teeth at the feeling of his steel being gripped by the inner muscles of Paris' vagina. This was one of the best feelings he had ever felt in his life and he planned to feel it the rest of his life.

Paris wrapped her arms around his neck and held on to him tightly all the while moaning his name. Yaseer kept pumping his steel until he felt he was about to cum, then he pulled out and turned her around. Paris already knew the drill as she bent toward the floor to touch her toes. She moaned out Yaseer's name when she felt him enter her again. He placed his left hand on the right side of her hip and he started hitting it from the back like a mad man. He tore into her real good making sure not to miss a spot. By the time he finished, both he and Paris was as limp as a noodle.

"Payback's a bitch, ain't it?" Yaseer thought to himself with a smile as he tried to catch his breath.

Yaseer woke up the next morning ready to get on his grind. Just because he was rich didn't mean he stopped hustling and making moves for his family. Paris was knocked out, so Yaseer gave her a kiss before he went to shower.

After showering, he threw on some blue and black basketball shorts, a pair of all black J's, a black T-shirt along with his TTC chain, and then he left out for the day.

He hopped in his whip and rolled the window down so that he could enjoy the fresh spring air that March had brought in. He turned up *Touchdown* by Yo Gotti and sped out of his brick driveway.

He made one stop after another, checking out all of his businesses and trap spots. When he got to the last stop on his agenda, Yaseer saw his workers out there playing around with some hoes instead of grinding.

He was pissed.

These niggas can play with pussy on their own time, not mine!

Yaseer hopped out of his ride and stormed over to the man who was in charge of that particular spot. "So, this how you let shit go down when I'm not around? You let muthafuckas play on my fuckin' time and money?" he asked.

"I didn't think it was a problem. They was just talking to the bitches."

This man had to be a dummy to respond to a stone cold killer like that. Yaseer decided it was time for him to see what he did to muthafuckas who thought they had time to talk to coochie while on the clock.

Yaseer went over to the one he knew as

Tristan. The young man didn't even know danger was approaching him because he was all up in a female's grill, not paying attention to what was going on and neither was the stupid fool beside him. Otherwise, he would have warned his boy.

Yaseer snatched his tool out of his shoulder holster as he got close to Tristan. Once he was right behind him, he tapped him on the shoulder. As soon as Tristan turned around, Yaseer plastered his brains all over shorty's face and clothes. Then he turned to the idiot that was beside the man he'd just shot and did him just as dirty. He didn't care that it was broad daylight, he had the police in his pocket and there was no one out there who was brave enough to snitch. Plus, he looked out for them, so he wasn't worried about getting locked down.

Yaseer walked back over to the nigga who he had left in charge, looked him in the eyes and said, "You see them buried niggas right there? Let me come back around here and niggas playin' around with coochie on my time and you will be the next one I put in the ground. Play with it if you want to. Get that shit cleaned up," Yaseer said, referring to the guys he had just sent to hell.

He didn't even give him time to respond.

Yaseer walked over to his car, got in, and pulled off. He had more important things to do, like finding out who was after him. Ezra had called him to tell him he had some info for him. Yaseer told him to meet him at his club called Day 1.

Yaseer walked in and spotted Ezra already there sitting in the V.I.P section, spitting game at one of the strippers. Yaseer shook his head and smirked. His boy was a trip. Ezra knew he loved him some pussy. Yaseer walked over toward where he was. As soon as Ezra spotted him, he met him halfway, dapping Yaseer up as soon as he got close enough.

"What's good wit ya, Yas?" Ezra asked.

"Everything sweet my way," he spoke as they both sat down on the plush, suede, royal blue couch. "So, what you got for me 'cause I know you ain't call me out here to just chop it up?"

"You right about that. Look, I don't know how to tell you this but look, you know that reward you had us put out?" Ezra asked.

Yaseer nodded his head up and down in response.

"Well, this lil' broad I used to fuck with over in Hidden Valley said she been hearing on the streets that *that* nigga Kameron over there on West Blvd. feeling some type of way because all his customers been coming our way. Now my question is, ain't that the same nigga that Kai'yan be kicking it with?"

Yaseer pondered for a moment before he responded to him.

"Yes," Yaseer finally stated. "But you honestly can't be implying that Kai'yan had something to do with me and Paris gettin' shot at. Do you know how long Kai and I have known each other? I have never spotted a disloyal bone in his body. You got to give me a lil' more proof than the word of a freak that you bang off and on," Yaseer said, giving him the side eye for even pointing his finger at his mans like that.

"Hit me up once you got more concrete evidence, bruh," he tacked on as he got up to leave.

Before Yaseer could even step an inch, Ezra grabbed his arm. Yaseer looked down at him with an expression that could kill the walking dead. No one put their hands on Yaseer with that much emphasis behind it, unless they were ready to lose their soul. Ezra caught his mistake and pulled his hand back. Then he reached inside his leather jacket and threw some photos on the table.

"Is that enough proof?" he spat.

Yaseer looked him up and down, letting him know without even speaking that if he pulled that again he would be dead. Yea, he and Ezra were close. But right now, until he knew who was really after him, everybody looked suspicious. For one, it never took him long at all to find out who had beef with him or wanted him dead.

Second of all, his boys on the street would have told him if it was Kameron, unless he had fools shook, which Yaseer doubted since he was the one who had the Queen City in a chokehold. Third, he was taught to beware of the dog bringing the bone to you. However, out of curiosity, he scooped the photos up off the table that sat in front of the couch in the VIP. Yaseer cast his eyes down at the photos. As he went through the photos, he got slightly heated on the inside. They were pictures of Kai'yan and Kameron in deep conversation together, exchanging money, etc. Yaseer put the photos inside his jacket for later use.

"I guess you looking for an apology for me doubting you, huh?" Yaseer said, looking Ezra in the eyes.

"Nah, you don't owe me no apologies. I knew you would doubt me, that's why I had the photos already on deck."

"One question before I bounce, how did you get those frames, son?"

Yaseer asked referring to the photos.

"I have my ways. I had to make sure I came correct since I would be implicating someone close to us who was in cahoots with a wanna be hustla to bring you down and take ya crown," answered Ezra.

"Thanks, my dude," Yaseer replied. Then he walked out of his establishment.

On his way to his car, Yaseer's phone started to vibrate. He pulled it out, looked at the caller I.D., pressed ignore, and put it back in his pocket. He didn't feel like talking to Ariel. He only had two reasons to ever be around or talk to her. And she didn't fall in either category right then and there.

Chapter 8

As soon as Yaseer left Day 1, he decided to do a "no call, show up." Just like jobs had "no call, no show" policy, he had his own which basically meant he didn't give any kind of notice that he was coming, he just appeared.

Yaseer pulled up to his rental agency which he had named Y&P Rental Agency. It was a two-story building that resembled a mini mansion. The bottom was the business and on the top was one of Yaseer's many trap spot's. Unless you knew the codes to access the room doors, you would never know what was being held inside any of the rooms on the top floor. Yaseer walked inside, nodded at the secretary, and kept on strolling. He walked over to the elevator that was located in the hallway, pressed the ascend button, and waited for the doors to open.

Once he had made it to the second floor as soon as he stepped off of the elevator, he heard

Kai'yan going off. Now, for him to be upset and yelling meant someone had really pissed him off. Kai'yan was a laid back type of dude who only raised his voice when he felt the need. And right about now, he obviously felt like this was one of those times that he needed to raise his voice.

"Where the fuck is the rest of my gwap?" Yaseer heard Kai'yan ask.

Yaseer stood at the bottom step unnoticed. He just wanted to observe.

"I-I-I swear I'ma have yo money to you by the end of the day, ju-just give me some more time," Yaseer heard the dude he knew as Jabo say.

"Nigga, this the second time you done came up in here short. I thought after the pistol whoopin' I served yo ass last time, you would have learned yo lesson. But obviously not, so yo time is up," Kai'yan said. Then he took his .22 and blew dude's last memory out of his head.

Yaseer started clapping as he stepped off of the bottom step. "Now that's how you handle that shit! That's what the fuck I'm talkin' 'bout," Yaseer said, hitting Yan on his back and showing all thirty-two of his teeth. "Now all you lil' rookies take note 'cause the next time either one of you come up in TTC shit short, yo ass will not go as easy. I will come and personally haul yo ass down to the chambers and peal the muthafuckin' flesh off of your bones. Now get this shit face out of my place of business," Yaseer said to no one in particular, knowing that they would all move at once to try and appease him. And sure enough, they all tried to move at once.

"Kai'yan, take a ride with me. I got some shit I need to speak with you about," Yaseer said and turned to walk out. He knew his so-called boy wouldn't be too far behind him.

Yaseer took his jacket off once he stepped outside. It was beginning to warm up. He was beyond happy that winter was almost gone. They got in Yaseer's car and pulled off. Yaseer had to be cautious when he approached this subject because if

Kai'yan wasn't trying to set him up, he was going to feel dumb, especially if he jumped too soon and blew his fuckin' head off.

"You been having meetings with Kameron?" Yaseer asked, jumping right into what he needed to speak with him about. There was no easy way to approach the subject besides just jumping in it head first.

"Yea," Kai'yan answered.

"So what y'all plotting? Y'all tryna take me down?" Yaseer hated to have to speak to his boy that way but that was a part of surviving and being a Boss.

Kai'yan looked at Yaseer sideways, like he had just lost his last brain cell.

"Did you really just ask me some bullshit like that? You questioning my loyalty like I'm one of these synthetic niggas. I wonder where you got that information from."

"Look, I gotta check any shit that come by me about who had the balls to come aiming at my dome, especially when I'm looking at shit like this," Yaseer replied, taking the photos out of his jacket and tossing them in Kai'yan's direction.

Kai'yan looked through the photos with an expressionless face. Then, out of nowhere, burst out laughing like Eddie Murphy himself had come and told him one of his *Delirious* jokes.

Now Yaseer was the one thinking that his boy was losing his last brain cell, laughing at a time like this. Slowly but surely, Kai'yan's laughter died down.

"Damn son, if you gon' have fools following me taking snap shots, make sure they at least get my best side, got a nigga in this photo looking blacker than muhfuckin' Wesley Snipes gums. Oh yea, and make sure they attach some microphones so you can hear what is being said. While you thinking I was trying to set you up, I was over here paying muhfuckas to keep their ears to the street. Me and Kam go back to when I first came down to this joint. Plus, he owes me a favor. That nigga ain't got no beef with you, but right about now I'm feeling dumb salty for you even questioning my get down like a bitch when I done had yo back all day every day since day one. You know how my parents went down. So that's like a slap in my face for you to even come at me like that."

"Listen, son, I'm just trying to figure out who after me. Don't nobody send goons after you shooting like that unless they want you dead. Now someone had to tell them we was all stepping out because it was a last minute choice. I hated to come at you like that but it is what it is. And by the way, I didn't have anyone take those photos of you. Someone brought those to me. Look, you know saying sorry ain't my style and it would also be a lie if I said it because I ain't sorry for trying to find my next victim. In situations like these, you got to stay on yo toes. I got love and mad respect for you. But until the truth is revealed, I can't sit and honestly apologize until I know for sure that you were falsely accused," Yaseer said to Kai'yan. He knew it sounded fucked up but he wasn't about to sugarcoat shit.

Kai'yan just nodded his head.

"If I find out that the person who pointed the finger pointed it the wrong way, I will personally let you cut that finger off. Now I need to go clear my head, so I'm 'bout to drop you back off at the spot and I will be M.I.A for the rest of the day. But you know to call me if it's an emergency." Yaseer ended the conversation with that. He knew Kai'yan was upset so he wouldn't have too much of anything to say to him for these next few days, but that was cool. Yaseer knew if it was him, he would probably be pissed, too. Yaseer dropped him back off and all but raced home to Paris. He needed to feel love from the only person he knew who kept it real with him.

Chapter 9

Yaseer pulled up to the crib and rushed upstairs to his reason for living. He walked in their bedroom and stopped to admire her for a brief moment. There she sat, glasses perched on the tip of her nose in red boy shorts, black footies, a black baby tee with her hair in a ball on the top of her head.

"Damn, my baby looking sexy as hell," Yaseer thought to himself.

She was reading one of the many books she owned called *Pussy Trap 3* by one her favorite authors, NeNe Capri. Yaseer casually strolled over to Paris, ready to spend some time loving on her. He climbed in the bed and lay down beside her.

"Hey, sugar, can ya man get some love and affection?" he asked.

"Of course you can. You know you can get that anytime you want it," she stated, leaning over giving him a deep passionate kiss. "I'm glad you're here. I had something I wanted us to do that we have not done since I have been home. I been home for a few weeks now and I have been dying for us to do this. Sooo, with that being said, I went and bought us some of our old favorite board games Yahtzee, Scrabble, and Monopoly, you choose," she said, getting up and preparing to get them.

"Monopoly, girl you know I like that cash monneeyy," Yaseer sang out in his best Rich Homie Quan voice with a grin on his face.

"Oh, shit, yo ass tryna be brave coming up against the Queen of Mula?" she said with a smirk.

"Hell yeah, a nigga bout to take your title and crown, then crown my own damn self the King."

"Aanndd you talking shit, let me whoop that ass right quick and take ya bread, and we ain't playing with fake money so get ya knot ready to be peeled," she replied.

Yaseer had to chuckle. His girl was a true hustla, just like her man. "Sshheeiitt, you ain't said

91

nothing but a word," he replied.

Paris went and got the game, and then went to the safe and pulled out four stacks. Anytime they played Monopoly, they used real money instead of fake, it made it more exciting. Toward the end of the game, when Paris saw that she might lose, she started playing dirty and taking off clothing items. Her shirt was first. Any man in his right mind would get distracted, especially a hot-blooded male like Yaseer.

"See, you ain't right. Don't think you 'bout to get me off my square 'cause you stripping to keep from losing," Yaseer spat as he threw the dice, and then cheered when he landed on boardwalk. It was on the only property he needed.

Now he owned all the greens, the yellows, and the orange properties. He also owned the railroads as well as had hotels on his other properties. So yeah, he had a lot of Paris' money and was about to get the rest of her change with Boardwalk and Park Place. When he looked up to give her the dice, his jaw dropped. Paris had taken off her bra and her shorts, and was now sitting in front of him with only a royal purple see through thong on.

"Oh shit," was the only words he could think of.

Paris smiled. She knew she had him by the balls. Yaseer dropped the dice and brushed his money aside. He climbed over the board game to her and used his body to lay her back. Then he used his knee to part her caramel colored thighs.

Yaseer lowered his face to hers and said, "You know you ain't right."

"What I do?" Paris responded with an innocent expression on her face.

"Oh, so now you ain't did nothing, then why my dick rocked up and I'm between your thighs? Not to mention, that's the only part of you that's even semi-covered and that I abandoned my money."

Paris had to smile at her own antics. She

knew she had played dirty but she refused to lose.

"You know I'm going to make you pay for that," Yaseer whispered as he kissed her and then proceeded to take off the last stitch of clothing she had on. He began to slowly move his pelvis back and forth, grinding into her twat and making her beg to feel him stretch her wide. But he wasn't done teasing her yet.

Yaseer moved lower, bringing his head face to face with her golden paradise. He began swiping at the kitty with teasing swipes. Then he started going in faster and deeper, tongue to tongue, lips to lips. Paris began to ride his face from below. Yaseer could tell from the faces Paris was making that she was ready to explode. So as soon as she was right there about to let go, he purposely pulled back and started kissing on her inner thighs.

She attempted to push his head back down, but to no avail.

Yaseer looked up and said with a smirk, "Pay back a mutha, ain't it?"

"Yyyaa-ssss-ss Yasseerr I'm ssooorryy. Please, I need to feel you," she whined.

"Say I won."

"Okaayy, you woonn! Now stop playing and make love to me. I need you," she pleaded out to him.

Yaseer peeled off his clothes. Then inch by inch, he inserted his member deeper and deeper inside of the place that had become his home. He was glad to be there. That night they made love with every fiber in their bodies. It was like they were on another level and neither one of them wanted to come down.

Later on that night, Yaseer and Paris were chilling in bed, laughing and joking, when his phone started going off. He picked up the phone to look at the caller I.D. "Fuck," he muttered under his breath. There was no way he could take the call in front of Paris so he ignored the call.

"Who was that, bae? I barely see you ignore calls," Paris questioned.

"It was Ezra calling. I'll call him back later. I just want to sit here and relax with the future Mrs. Davis. I'm pretty sure whatever he has to tell me can wait."

"The future Mrs. Davis, huh? I been meaning to speak with you about that. But with everything going on, I didn't want to bother you with it. But since we are on the subject, when do you think we can make it official?" she asked, peering up at Yaseer with the most beautiful eyes he had ever seen.

"When you want to make it official?" he replied as he pulled her naked body closer to his.

"I'm ready whenever you are. I can't wait to be Mrs. Yaseer Aleem Davis," she said with a wide smile, gazing down at her engagement ring.

Yaseer's heart swelled with joy. Despite everything going on, Yaseer refused to make Paris wait any longer.

"Let's do it tomorrow," Yaseer said, looking down at her in the crook of his chest and shoulder.

"Are you serious?" she inquired, sitting straight up in the bed and looking over at him, waiting for his response.

"Nah, I was just fucking with you. Let's wait a year before we make it official," Yaseer was trying his hardest not to crack up after letting that cruel joke flow through his lips. The grin on her face faded into a tiny smile.

"Girl, I'm just playing with you. Yes, I'm serious about getting married tomorrow," Yaseer said, finally giving in to his giggles.

"You play too damn much," she responded, attempting to be serious. But then she had to laugh at his shenanigans.

Yaseer's phone started to ring again, interrupting their laughter.

"Hold up for a sec, bae. Let me take this call. It must be important if E calling me again," Yaseer said while getting up to go take the call in another room. He knew Paris would find it odd that he was taking his call in another room, but he would have to find something to tell her. Yaseer walked into the room a few rooms down from their bedroom.

"This better be fuckin' important," he whispered into the receiver.

"I need to see you tomorrow," his caller responded.

"For what? Yo ass don't have a reason to see or call me unless it concerns two individuals. So unless they are hurt, sick, or etc. get the fuck off my phone and your request to see me tomorrow is denied," Yaseer spat nastily into the phone. *"I swear this bitch trapped me,"* he thought to himself.

"You need to spend some time with your seeds. Are you going to deny them, too?" she replied just as nastily.

"Bitch, don't play. You know I never would deny seeing my damn kids. I will pick them up tomorrow. Have them dressed and ready when I get there," Yaseer replied.

Yaseer hated that girl. The only reason she

was still alive was because she was the mother of his kids. He slipped up one time while Paris was away and ended up with two little ones after a one night stand from one his strippers at Day 1.

"Okay, I will have them ready when you get here," his baby momma responded.

Yaseer didn't even reply, he just hung up on her and stood there in place. He had to come clean with Paris but it was hard for him to even form the words to tell her.

"Yeah, I'm definitely marrying her tomorrow. At least if she finds out, we will already be married. Then it's 'til death do us part up in this bitch. I was fucking up everything I always boasted about. But now I see how a muthafucka could go back on his own words. I swear I hate every bit of this but I can't lose my world."

Yaseer stood there thinking to himself for a moment longer before putting his emotions in check. Then he came up with the best lie he could think of to explain why he took the call in another room. Yaseer hated the fact that he was becoming more and more of the type of person he despised every time he looked Paris in the face and didn't confess his mistake to her.

Yaseer strolled back into their bedroom, thankful that Paris was in the shower. He just prayed she stayed in the shower a long time as she usually did. Yaseer tip-toed to the bed, got in, and went to sleep as fast as he could. Tomorrow he planned to be up and out early as hell just so he could postpone the questions that he knew were sure to come.

The next morning, Yaseer was out of the house by 8AM. Paris was still knocked out.

"Thank you, God," Yaseer mumbled to himself.

He had everything planned out. He planned to have a note sent her for her to meet him later on at the airport. They would fly out to Las Ventanas, San Jose Del Cabo no later than 2PM and be husband and wife by the time the night was over.

He'd made the arrangements as soon as he got up that morning. He couldn't wait. He was hoping this would make her forget about his phone call last night.

She knew Yaseer never talked to Ezra in private. Being that she was a part of TTC, she already knew everything so Yaseer never had to talk in secret.

Yaseer went to Toys R Us to scoop up his little ones some toys. Then he drove over to Concord Mills to cop them some clothes and shoes. He loved his seeds he just hated he couldn't have them every day like he wanted to.

By 11:30AM, Yaseer was in front of Ariel's house. Yaseer called her to let her know he was outside.

"Bring 'em out," Yaseer said after she answered phone and then disconnected the call.

Yaseer knew he was being rude to her, but Ariel was sheisty. For starters, she was always trying to use his kids to see him, and she always had something slick to say out her mouth about Paris. She knew from the time she left the club with Yaseer until the time they went to her crib that it was only going to be sex, nothing more, nothing less. And she agreed.

That night, Yaseer had been feeling good off the alcohol and it had been almost a year since he had had some. He was horny and his hand wasn't getting it. He hadn't stepped out on Paris in years. But at that moment, he needed some and didn't think nothing would come of it.

Ariel had told him she was on birth control before he slid in. That made him disregard his number one rule: *Never raw dawg a female unless you plan on wifing her*. He should have stuck to the script.

Yaseer and Ariel were mad cool. And that night that they'd spent together made them a little friendlier. But Yaseer refused to have sex with her again. Not that her pussy wasn't good, because it was. But he felt foul after screwing another female while his girl was doing his bid, and he had sworn to himself that he would never step out on his girl again.

The next thing Yaseer knew, a month later, Ariel was coming to him telling him she was pregnant. Of course, he questioned her about her birth control, and she told him it must have failed.

So one day, Yaseer went to her house to take her some crackers and ginger ale for her morning sickness. He stepped in for a few, just to chill with her for a little bit, but she ended up falling asleep. Yaseer was about to leave but something told him to search her house to see if something was foul about Ariel getting knocked up by him. Something just didn't seem right about it.

The first place he searched was her bedroom. He was about to give up until he thoroughly went through her dresser drawer and found some birth control pills in the back of it. Yaseer almost threw them back in the drawer until he noticed the date on the package. It was dated a few weeks before they had slept together. Out of curiosity, he opened the pack to see if she had indeed been taking her birth control. Yaseer opened the pack and the shit was full, only two were missing. If she had been taking them on the regular, she would not have gotten pregnant.

Yaseer walked back into the living room to where she was sleeping, and went the fuck off.

"Bitch! Wake yo lying ass up!" Yaseer yelled.

She looked up at him groggily. Yaseer didn't give a fuck about her being sleepy. At this point, he was pissed off.

"Why are you yelling? Damn, Yaseer, couldn't you at least have let me finish my nap? Shit!" Ariel said while sitting up and wiping the sleep out of her eyes.

"You think I give a fuck about yo damn sleep? Why the fuck you lie to me about being on birth control before we fucked, you stupid hoe?"

Yaseer spat at her.

At first, she looked like she was in shock and then she started to smile. "You should have wrapped it up," she said with a smirk.

She was lucky she was pregnant with Yaseer's seeds. Otherwise, he would have put one in her skull.

"You triflin' bitch! I regret even aiming my dick anywhere near yo ass." Yaseer backed up to leave, making sure to tell her to never call him unless it concerning his unborn.

Less than a year later, he welcomed the arrival of not one, but two beautiful baby girls.

Yaseer honked the horn. Ariel needed to hurry up because he had things to do. She finally emerged from the house with his little ones in tote. Yaseer got out to open the car door so he could take them from her, strap them in their car seats, and go on about his business.

"Hello to you, too," Ariel said.

But he wasn't even trying to hear her. He grabbed his daughters' baby bags, put them in the car as well and then drove off, leaving Ariel standing in the driveway.

Chapter 10

Paris had received a note from Yaseer telling her to meet him for lunch at an address he had written on a card which came along with an assortment of different roses he had delivered from a flower company she absolutely adored.

She smiled glancing over at the small white card again that sat on the night stand. Yasser's hand writing looked sloppier than usual, but she chalked it up as him rushing.

Paris double-checked herself in the mirror to make sure she looked good. She had her hair pulled back into a low bun. She wore high waist jeans, a tight fitting black shirt that was cut low in the front and black thigh-high boots. Her gold diamond hoops brushed against her shoulder as she turned her head to smooth down her edges. She checked her makeup to make sure it was straight, grabbed her keys and Michael Kors bag, and left out to go meet Yaseer.

Paris got in her 2013 all-white Benz and pumped up August Alsina's smash joint *I Luv This Shit* as she sped out of the driveway. She was in her own world. As quiet as it's kept, out of the girls, Paris was the wildest one. But she knew when to wild out and when the fuck to chill.

Bitches used to stay trying her, especially through her high school years. She could clearly remember this hoe that stayed trying her named Sage. Every day she would always have something smart to say to her in class, in the hallways, lunch, or wherever she saw her. One day in particular, Paris wasn't feeling well. When school let out for the day and she was walking out of the building to go home, the bitch decided that day would be the day she would attempt to give Paris hell.

"Look at this bamma bitch, basic looking hoe," Sage mused around with her friends, making sure everyone heard her.

Paris kept walking, trying to ignore Sage's snide comments. Sage was walking behind her with

108

her crew, steady yapping her mouth, unaware of the beast she was awakening.

"Damn, she a ugly bitch and her weave fucked up! Bitch acting like that's her fuckin' hair and shit, knowing she got that hair down the block at Lucy's. Her or her sister ain't shit. Hell, I just fucked London's man last week. I hope she know it's my pussy she tasting when Kobe kissing her."

That was it. Paris didn't give a fuck about her talking smack on her, but her sister was off limits. She knew if London was there she would handle the hoe her damn self. But since she wasn't, she was about to handle the light work for her.

Paris turned around with her cool brown orbs boring into Sage's gray eyes. She threw her book bag down and stepped to Sage. Once she was close enough, she hit Sage with a mean right hook that sent Sage stumbling backwards. Paris took that moment to pounce on her and then commenced to whooping shawty's ass!

"Fuck you say, bitch? You been fuckin' with

me all day. Come on bitch! You bad, say something else hoe!" Paris yelled out while hurling hard blows on Sage's face that was now bloody. Paris stood up and starting stomping her and kicking her in the ribs.

"Say something now, bitch! Say. Another. Mutha. Fuckin'. Word. Hoe."

Sage's friends sat watching with their bottom jaw dropped open.

"Now when Kobe kiss you, I hope it's my fist he taste in your mouth, trick." Paris spat on her and mumbled, "Low budget hoe," as she picked her belongings up and finished walking home. Once there, she told London what happened.

London was only a year younger than Paris. She had stayed home that particular day because she wasn't feeling well. After hearing the part about ole girl fucking Kobe, London went berserk, sick and all. She called him, going off. He had the nerve to tell her that since her tight ass wasn't giving shit up, he had to get his dick wet somewhere. London told him it was all good because his brother, Jerrell, had been getting his dick wet by her every day for almost their entire six-month relationship. Although it was a lie, it felt good to hurt him as bad as he'd hurt her.

After hanging the phone up, she told Paris she was glad she had kicked the dusty hoe's ass.

Paris drove to the address she had been given, bobbing to the music she was playing and singing along with August Alsina.

"So I'ma keep on drinking cause I luv this shit/ And I'ma keep on smoking cause I luv this shit/And I'ma keep on grindin' cause I luv this shit..."

She continued singing while driving down the highway. Twenty minutes later, she pulled up to a nice one-story house. She was confused because this did not resemble a restaurant. Paris was about to pull up behind the vehicle she knew as Yaseer's when she saw something that made her pump her breaks.

There was a woman standing outside with him, beside his car. Paris watched as the woman handed over the most adorable little baby girl, and then she watched as she handed Yaseer another one, who was just as cute. Paris watched Yaseer put the girls in the car, take their baby bags, and pull off.

Paris' mind was traveling all over the place with one main question in mind. *Who were those babies and who was the tramp handing them off to him?*

Paris put her car into drive and followed his car, making sure to stay a few cars behind. She watched him turn into a restaurant that she and Yaseer visited on the regular. She circled the block twice, giving him enough time to get settled in before she pulled into the restaurant, parked her car, and was out in flash, after making sure to secure the locks on her car.

The waitress greeted her as she walked in, "Welcome to Jesani's, Ms. Jacobs. How are you doing today?" she asked Paris all happy and bubbly.

"I'm doing just fine, I'm here to meet Yaseer," Paris responded.

"He just arrived. Follow me." She motioned with her hand as she turned to lead her.

Paris followed her to a private room toward the back of the restaurant. Once they were close to the room, she tapped the waitress on the shoulder. The waitress stopped to hear what Paris was about to tell her.

"I think I can take it from here. I want to sneak up on him. I'm kinda early."

"No problem, enjoy your meal."

Paris quietly walked the rest of the way to the room where Yaseer was with the two little girls. One was crawling on the floor, playing with baby toys, and the other one he had standing up on his lap bouncing her up and down.

"Say da-da, da-da," she heard him say.

Paris was rooted in her spot. She felt the tears stinging the back of her eyes. She wanted to believe that she had heard wrong, but she had excellent hearing. She sucked in her emotions and strolled over to him.

"Hey, Daddy," she said as she approached him.

Yaseer ceased all movement the moment he heard his fiancée's voice. He moved the infant out of his view so he could see Paris. Yaseer looked as though he had seen a ghost.

"Bae, wh-what are you doing here?" Yaseer asked.

"I received your note, telling me to meet you at this address," she said, holding up the card so he could read it before tearing up the note and tossing the remains in his direction. A befuddled look came across Yasser's face for a split second. "Well, now, these are some beautiful little girls. Whose babies are they? I never took you as the babysitting type, especially since you have been denying giving me a baby," Paris stated. She had to see if Yaseer would lie to her. She had to at least see if he was man enough to tell her that they were his. She just had to hear him tell her himself that they were his seeds. But she didn't have to wait long.

"Sit down, Paris. I need to talk to you about some shit."

"I would rather stand."

"Sit down!" Yaseer growled, looking her right in the face with tears on the brim of each eye threatening to fall at any moment.

Paris sat down just to hear the crap that he was going to say to her. Right now, she couldn't care less. She already had in her head that she was leaving him, and there was nothing he could say to change that decision.

"I ain't 'bout to sit here and front, this shit been eating me up day and night, not telling you. But I didn't want to lose you, so I tried to keep everything a secret," he said, sitting the baby down on his left leg and picking the other child up, placing her on his right leg.

"These two princesses are my seven-month-old twin daughters. The bitch wasn't even supposed to get pregnant. She swore up and down she was on birth control. I had been drinking, I was horny, and I slipped up. But I swear to you on everything I love that was the only time I stepped out in years. I ended up finding out the hoe didn't even take her birth control prior to us messing around. Then a month later, she tells me she is pregnant."

Yaseer stopped a moment to swallow the lump in his throat and then continued on, "I didn't expect for you to find out like this. I had planned to tell you in another way, when the time was right. I'm so, so sorry, Paris. I swear I am. I just didn't know how to tell you."

"Thank you for at least being man enough to not lie to me and tell me the truth. Now, if you'll excuse me, I need to leave," Paris said, standing up and trying to hold her tears in until she got in her car. But as soon as she blinked, tears started to flow down her face.

She turned and rushed out of the restaurant,

leaving Yaseer screaming her name. Paris all but ran to her car, cranked it up, and zoomed out of the parking lot like a mad woman. How she made it home, she had no clue. Her body was literally on autopilot.

Paris walked in the house fuming. She immediately headed straight for the bedroom. She needed to get her shit and leave before Yaseer showed up because she couldn't deal with him right now. Otherwise, she wouldn't be responsible for anything that she might do. She automatically went to their closet and started slinging shit out.

"After all the shit I have done for his ass, this the thanks I get. In the five years we been together, I never cheated and was nothing but loyal. I did a bid for his ass, muthafucka. I gave my life and freedom for him and I'm still risking it for him every day when I leave out this house just because I'm his girl."

She saw him being there for his daughters' birth in her head and she felt her heart breaking

117

more and more. "Fuck him. I'm done." Paris kept yelling and tossing her shit out of the closet at the same time.

*****

Yaseer grabbed Chaunte and Madison's baby bags and rushed out of the restaurant faster than lightning. As soon as he had them secure in their car seats, he opened his car door, threw the bags in the passenger seat, and sped off. He dropped the girls back off at Ariel's house. Then he made his way home to try to salvage his relationship.

"God, please don't let her leave me," he prayed out loud, hoping that He would hear his prayers. Even though he didn't do right, he believed that God still had love for him because God was the one that created him.

Yaseer pulled up to his house, parked directly in front of his door, and was out in two point nine seconds.

"Paris! Paris!" Yaseer screamed, frantically

running upstairs, hoping that she was still there. As he got closer, he heard music playing and her going off at the same time.

Yaseer entered his room and spotted his clothes all over the floor. Any other time, he would have been pissed because Paris knew he hated a messy room and he definitely didn't like his expensive things on the floor. But seeing that he was the cause of her doing this, he calmed down real quick. The clothes, the house, or himself didn't mean shit if he didn't have his girl.

"Bae," Yaseer called out as he made long strides over to her to try to fix what he had broken. "Bae," Yaseer called out again, attempting to reach out to touch her.

"Don't touch me! Don't you dare put your fuckin' hands anywhere near me, Yaseer!" she yelled and then turned around to face him.

Yaseer felt as though his heart had been shattered into a million pieces when she turned around and he saw the expression and tears on her face. He had broken something that was truly priceless. Yaseer wanted to break down on his knees, knowing that this might be the end for them. He just couldn't see life without Paris. She had taken him as he was, and she never judged him or anything. All that she asked was for him not to hurt her, and he gave her his word.

"Just how long did you plan to keep this hidden from me? How long did you think you could keep going before I found out the truth? Did you ever intend on telling me? Huh? Answer me got damnit!" Paris screamed at Yaseer hysterically.

He was speechless. What could he say?

He couldn't even honestly say how long it would have taking him to tell her. In a way, he felt he didn't lie he just never told her so he couldn't say that he was sorry for lying to her. He was not sorry about his daughters, but he was sorry that she is not their blood mother.

"I fucked up, okay! I fucked up! How was I supposed to tell you? Huh? Was I supposed to tell you at visitation when you were doing my bid? Was I supposed to tell you the moment you were happy to be able to have your freedom back? Or how about when I was deep in the pussy? Or maybe over dinner? You tell me when would it have been the right time that would not have landed us in the situation we are in now," Yaseer snapped. He was angrier at himself than anything.

"How the fuck did she know where to come? The note I had sent her said to meet me at the airport at 1:30. How in the hell did she know where Ariel lived. The only person who knew that I was spending time with the girls today was Liam and that's because he was supposed to be meeting me. Something is not right! Once I find out who is responsible for my girl finding out about my babies in this way, I am going to snap their fucking neck and then blow their brains out of the opposite end that my bullet entered their skull." Yaseer mulled over in his head. He swiped his hand over his face to try to calm his emotions. He was about to

apologize when something went flying past his face.

"Did shorty just throw something at me?" Yaseer questioned under his breath. Yaseer looked back to see what Paris had thrown. *"When the hell did she pick up a heel? She threw that shit like a MLB player. Fuck, ma is going all the way in,"* Yaseer thought as he stood motionless, trying to figure out his next move.

"Fuck you, Yaseer! Fuck you! Fuck you!"

She broke down crying. She felt as though the life was being sucked right out of her. How could she stay with a man who would hurt her this deeply? She didn't expect him not to cheat at least once. She never fooled herself into believing that. She wasn't naive to the fact the he was a man and a man was going to do what a man was going to do, but why when your girl was doing *your* time? But for him to fuck around and not strap the fuck up, and then get the bitch pregnant with not only one, but two children, like she didn't mean shit made her feel less than a woman. She couldn't comprehend how a man of his caliber could be so foolish.

Yaseer reached out to her again. She tried to push him back and started hitting his chest, but eventually she stopped fighting and let him pull her into his embrace.

"Honey dip," he called her affectionately by the nickname he had given her some years back.

Yaseer picked her up in his arms, carried her over to the bed, and climbed in beside her. He pulled her closer to his body and began placing soft kisses down her neck as his hand eased down the waistband of her panties and went straight for her love spot.

"Forgive me," he whispered pleadingly in her ear. "I'm so sorry for causing you so much pain. Baby, I'm sorry. I love you. Say you will forgive me. Say you will," he said barely above a whisper in Paris' ear as he put two fingers inside of her and began working her until she started to moan and cry at the same time.

"Why? Yaseer, why?" Paris asked. The

music was playing softly, and as if on cue, *Next Breath* by Tank started crooning through the speakers.

I'm sorry for the times that I stressed you out/and I'm thankful for the times you ain't put me out your house/ I fell in love more than once but every single time it was with you girl/ I don't think I've ever/ ever really told you how much I need you/ I need you more than my next breath/never will I ever leave you cause darling I need you/ I need you more than the next breath I breathe...

She looked in his eyes and Yaseer couldn't help but feel the love she had for him. No matter how bad he had injured her soul, he assumed she would never leave him, and vice versa. He had no answer for her question. There was nothing he could say. He wished he would have stayed strong and kept his penis in his pants. But then again, he was only human.

Paris kept her eyes trained on him and all he could do was be honest and pour out his heart and pray that that would be enough.

"I fucked up bad, baby. I will spend the rest of my life telling you I'm sorry and trying to make up for the pain I have caused in your heart. Baby, please just keep working with me. I promise I will do whatever it takes to repair the heart that I damaged and made fragile while in the care of my hands," Yaseer responded, kissing her passionately.

Tears streamed down both of their faces from hurt, broken promises, and love. Yaseer kept on with his deadly assault of love, kissing his way down his soul's body and making his way to her love portal.

Once he reached his destination, he went to work proving his love to the woman who had his heart in a vice grip.

"Aaahhhh, Yaseer, I'm about to cccuummm!" Paris screamed out from the sweet torture he was bestowing upon her.

"Let me have it, my queen," was his response.

With those words, he received one of the sweetest treats only Paris' body could produce for him. He felt her body begin to tremble but he refused to let up. Instead, Yaseer gripped her thighs and feasted on her love spot as if it was his last meal and he was starved. By the time he finished, she was weak. But that didn't mean a thing. Yaseer removed his boxers and dived straight into the spot that would one day bear his seeds. From the way he was going, she would be bearing his seed soon.

Yaseer kept pounding, ensuring that his thrust were deep and strong. Soon Yaseer was coming along with Paris while whispering promises of love in her ear and apologizing for all that he had done. They made love all throughout the night.

The next morning, Yaseer woke up upon feeling Paris' spot empty beside him. Something wasn't right and he could feel it. Paris rarely woke up before him. He immediately jumped up and went through the house, looking for Paris. Then he started to notice along the way that some of her belongings were gone.

He rushed back upstairs to their room to where the clothes she had thrown on the floor the night before still remained. Yaseer walked over to them to look at the place in the closet where she normally kept her luggage. They were gone. Every single bag. Yaseer sped back downstairs. As soon as he got to the bottom of the stairs and prepared to grab his keys off of the end table by the door, he spotted a note. Yaseer scooped the note up to read it.

It simply read: *I can't do this anymore. Love, Paris.*

He felt like he was about to start hyperventilating. She had left him. His heart was gone. He knew he had messed up. But after last night, he figured she was going to try to work things out with him.

Yaseer felt the need to hit something, and since no one was around that he could do bodily harm to, he used the wall as his target. Yaseer drove his fist into the wall like Mike Tyson used to drive his fist into his opponent's face.

"Fuck!" Yaseer screamed out with tears racing down his face.

He slid down the wall, making his knees meet the floor. He broke down crying harder than a bride who had just got stood up at the altar in front of all of her friends and family.

"I got to fix this. I can't live without my heart," Yaseer cried out. He stood up, wiped his eyes, grabbed his car keys, and rushed out of the door.

"This bitch wanted to try and be fucking funny. How else would Paris have known her address?" he wondered. But he had something for her ass. He got in his car and pulled off. He cranked up DJ Drama and Future's joint and sang the lyrics.

A bitch gone be a bitch/ A hoe gone be a hoe/ A killer gone be a killer/ That's sumthin' you need to know/ Ain't no way around it, ain't no way around it.

How ironic the lyrics were. Even the people on the radio knew how he was feeling about this bitch. He knew for sure he was going to have to turn shorty loose after this because the bitch didn't know her muthafuckin' place. Look at the drama she just caused. Now he was going to have to do something that he should have done a long time ago and that was to stop having sex with her.

Chapter 11

Yaseer pulled up in front of Ariel's house. He had placed her in a real nice house. It was all one level but it sat on an acre of land. He had her living in Ballantyne, NC out there with the bougie people. She didn't even have to stay in the hood. All she had to do is sit back, take care of his seeds, and live comfortably.

Yaseer opened the door and went straight for the room where he knew she would be waiting. He opened the door only to find her laid out on the bed butt ass naked with her legs cocked wide open and her fingers deep inside her pussy.

Yaseer rocked up at the image. Her sun-kissed golden skin did something to him every time, and the fact that she was thick didn't help matters either.

He had to check his dick so he could handle

her accordingly. He walked over to the bed and peered over her.

"Shit," he mumbled to himself. Her 38DD's were eying him, begging to be touched. Again he checked his dick.

"Ariel!"

"Yes, Daddy," she answered, looking at him from between her slanted shaped eyelids. Her honey-colored eyes were mesmerizing. Right about now, from the way she was looking at him, he was ready to pause his words and put in work. But that would have to wait because the bitch had gotten out of bounds and fucked with the home front.

"Did you send your address to Paris in a note, making her think I wanted her to meet me here? You know what, don't answer that 'cause I don't wanna hear the lie you 'bout to tell. I guess you thought I was joking when I threatened to feed your ass to my pits, huh? Okay. I got something for your ass."

Yaseer whistled and in walked the two

biggest pit bulls Ariel had ever seen. Her eyes looked as though they were going to pop out of their sockets. When she turned to look at Yaseer, he had his .45 aimed at her dome. She about pissed herself.

"I-I-I did-didn't ha-" Ariel told Yaseer.

"Save yo lies, hoe. Now try to play me for a fool again and your ass will be kibbles and bits. Fuck with me if you want, bitch. This your last warning. The only reason you are not their meal right now is because you're the mother of my kids. But try me again and they won't have a fuckin' mother."

Ariel nodded as she sat up on her haunches with the gun still aimed at her head. She took her hands, unzipped his pants, pulled out his ten inches, and pushed him as far as she could down her throat. His gangster had turned her freakiness up to a hundred.

Yaseer looked at her through lowered eyes and thought, *"Damn, this bitch a straight freak."* He stilled her head with his hand and started moving his hips back and forth, fucking her mouth. The moment he felt that he was going to bust he pushed her back on the bed. Took off his clothes, retrieved a condom from his wallet, sheathed himself and then slid into her hard and rough.

There was nothing loving about this. It was a straight up fuck. No pleasure involved, it was about showing her that he was the wrong one to cross and to make her think twice before doing it again Yaseer flipped Ariel around on her hands and knees. He wrapped her silky strands around his hand, making a fist. Then he took all of himself and drove right in her virgin anus.

Ariel screamed from the pain of the unexpected intrusion. "Next time I tell you not to do something, you gon' listen?" he asked as he continued to pound away.

"Yy-eee-ssss," she cried out.

"I'm the boss of this shit. What I say go, no questions asked! You understand me, slut?" Yaseer was the truth. That's why she went crazy over him.

"Uh huh. Fuck me, Daddy. Harder. Harder." Her pain had turned into pleasure as the blood from her anal area became lubricant.

"This bitch a serious nympho and a pain freak!" Yaseer thought to himself as he kept drilling her ass. He bust hard as hell.

As soon as he was finished releasing in the condom, he pulled out of her and went to dispose of it. Yaseer walked back in the room and quickly dressed. Ariel sat watching him.

"You're leaving?" She said with a hint of an attitude.

"You questioning me? The fuck I just tell you about that? Take yo tired ass to sleep I'll be back when I feel the need. Now in the words of a job that ain't trying to hire a muthafucka, *'Don't call me, I will call you.'"*

With that, Yaseer walked out of the door, leaving his pits there to watch her every movement. He had to find out where Paris was and get her back.

134

*****

Paris sat in her hotel room crying. Out of all the things he could have done to her, this was by far the worst. She would have rather he kill her than to be feeling the pain in her heart that she felt now.

"Oh, God, I can't believe I sacrificed two years of my life for that bastard! Why did he have to do this to me?" Paris cried out on her knees in the hotel room.

She cried and cried to the point she felt like she was going to puke. Paris got up and flew to the bathroom faster than a jet, bent over the toilet, and gave up all of her stomach contents. What hurt her the most was not the fact that he cheated. She expected him to slip being that she was doing time. But to get the hoe pregnant was a whole different level. Then on top of that, to hold it from her instead of being up front and saying, 'Baby, I fucked up,' was like a slap in the face. To her it was worse than a hollow tip to the center of her cranium.

After she finished throwing up, she sat on the floor beside the toilet with her head in her hands. She felt like dying. Yaseer was her life and the only man she had ever loved or could see herself with. But how do you push something that big under the rug. She tried to rationalize it by thinking of the fact that she had her own secret, but to think of him having another woman's kids seemed worse than what could ever come out about her. All she wanted was a child. Although she didn't verbalize it, she was sure he knew that as well. Unbeknownst to him, she had stopped taking her birth control pills. But now she was regretting it big time. Yeah, she had slept with him last night. But at that moment, her emotions were every damn where.

For the life of her she couldn't comprehend how he could constantly speak about loyalty, honesty, and respect when he couldn't even respect her enough to be honest with her about getting this popcorn hoe fucking pregnant.

"I hate him," she falsely choked out between

sobs. Then she took the cheap bottle of shampoo that was on the edge of the tub and threw it across the bathroom. "Fuck him!" she screamed out.

She needed a break from the world and she was determined to have one. But how long could she go without yearning for the love of her life?

Knock! Knock! Knock!

Paris' head whipped up at the sound of someone knocking at the door. She wiped her face, snot and all, with the back of her hand. Then she stood up to go see who was at the door.

"Who the fuck at the door? Don't nobody know where the hell I'm at," Paris thought.

Paris swung the door open with her gat in hand, ready for whatever. She was a little taken aback when she saw that her visitor was Yaseer's boy.

"What are you doing here? Matter of fact, how did you even know where I was?" Paris questioned her visitor while taking a step back to let him in. She walked over to sit on the bed after placing her gun on the end table. "I hope you not here to plead your boy's case, 'cause if so, you might as well take yo high yella ass right back out that door to Yaseer and tell him I said fuck 'em while you at it," Paris said with venom dripping from every word.

Her visitor walked over to where she sat on the edge of the bed, making sure to grab himself a chair from the table by the window in the process. He positioned his chair to sit directly in front of her so that he could look her right in the eyes.

"Look, I ain't even 'bout to sit here and act like that shit he did was all gucci because it wasn't. That's the reason I had that note sent to you so you could see everything with your own eyes. I fe—"

"Wait, wait, wait, hold the hell on, so you're the reason my life is in shambles now?" Paris asked her visitor, ready to go in on him.

"Yes, I felt like you deserved to know the truth. Yaseer is always talking about loyalty, honesty, and respect, but where were his values when he was fuckin' that hoe while you did his bid?" How did you even know he had a side family?" Paris questioned.

"I was on my way to see my girl and that's when I saw him dropping some shorties off to this fine dime brizzal. I couldn't sleep knowing the truth and then turn around, cheesing in your face. Now look, here is the thing, I want to help you turn all this shit back around on him because I no longer feel that he is a man of his word. I think you deserve some payback. I have seen your get down. I know you loyal to the bone, but I know this shit got you feeling some type of way."

Paris cringed on the inside. She was mad as hell at Yaseer but there was no way in hell she could ever see herself flipping on him. Yeah, he fucked up real bad. But deep down inside, she knew after all of this, she wasn't going to leave him permanently. Her instincts had been telling her all along that this nigga sitting in front of her was foul. She could smell a snake a mile away. *Hell*, her own daddy was one, which was why she despised his ass. She decided to ask him one more question before she went ham on him.

"What will you get out of this?" Paris asked the man in front of her.

"Satisfaction. The satisfaction of seeing his ass hurt like he has hurt others," he replied.

Paris laughed and then turned to him and gave him one of her and Yaseer's favorite Kevin Hart lines.

"You are something else! Let me guess, you thought if you exposed the truth to me, I would be so hurt that I would help you? I wouldn't help you fuck Yaseer over with the next nigga's dick. Now get the fuck out of my damn room," Paris spewed out angrily while walking to the door to see her visitor out. She had only gotten the door halfway open before her visitor came up behind her and slammed the door shut with all of his strength, making the door slam loudly.

"Oh, you will help me, unless you want

Yaseer to find out the truth about your ol' man," he said as he pushed her against the door.

Paris wished she could reach her gun right now, but it was a little too late for that.

"How-how do you know about that?"

"You ain't as slick as you think, bitch. All it took was a little research. I was looking for information on ya man when I came across that little info on you," her unwanted visitor hissed between his teeth.

Paris knew she was fucked but she had to make it out of there today so that she could at least be the first person to tell Yaseer the truth about her sperm donor.

"London knows where I'm at. If you know Yaseer like I do, then you know he has already questioned her about my whereabouts and you know she not 'bout to lie to him for me or anyone else. So if I were you I would just go ahead and leave now," Paris replied, hoping that the idea that Yaseer would possibly show up would scare him off, but not so. That only made shit worse.

"You think I give a fuck! Huh, bitch? Like he would believe shit that come out your mouth after I tell him the truth about you," her visitor said.

"How could you do this to him? You know he loves you like family and is beyond loyal to you, yet you're ready to kill him? I will not help you, so you might as well just kill me because I would rather go out as a gangsta bitch than a snake bitch any day," Paris spoke fearlessly calm to her visitor.

The only thing she feared was something happening to the love of her life. She prayed he would seek vengeance upon her death and find out that the man he trusted with his life is the man who is out to destroy and kill him by any means necessary, even if that included stooping as low as to solicit her help, which was exactly what he was doing now.

As soon as those last words flowed through Paris' lips her visitor spun her around with the swiftness of a cheetah, and punched her in her mouth. He then grabbed her by the throat, lifted her up, and slammed her into the door, knocking the wind out of her chest. He got real close to her face and looked her dead in the eyes with a chilling look on his face.

Between clenched teeth, he said to her, "Listen you stupid, bitch. You are going to help me with this plan whether you like it or not, or not only will I expose your dirt, that pretty little sister of yours will end up floating in a lake with missing body parts. You understand me. Now your attitude, plus the way you look, done got my dick hard. Since I know you won't give it to me, I'ma take it," her visitor stated and then yanked her black tights down and ripped the sides of her panties.

He pushed into her hard and rough, still holding her up in the air on the wall by her throat. Paris wanted to cry, but she refused do so in front of this monster. He kept pounding, not giving a damn that he was damn near ripping her body in two.

After a while, Paris was on the brink of

passing out from the pain of his forced intrusion as well as the fact that he was choking the life out of her.

After letting off inside of her, he threw her to the side like yesterday's trash and walked out, leaving her bleeding on the floor.

The last thing Paris remembered mumbling before blacking out was, "You should have killed me." Not only had he betrayed and disrespected Yaseer, he had also threatened a member of the crew and raped her. He should have known that there would be hell to pay for even laying a finger on Paris, let alone leaving her alive after doing so.

Chapter 12

Yaseer pulled up to the hotel and rushed to the room number he was given. He knew if no one else knew where his love was resting her head at, her sister would. When he got near the room, he felt a tightening in his gut. He had that feeling that once again something was wrong.

Yaseer all but ran the rest of the way to the room and as he got closer and closer noticed the door had been left ajar. Yaseer pushed the door open and his eyes immediately fell on Paris, sprawled out on the floor with blood coming from her mouth and nose, a handprint on her neck as if she had been choked to death, and last but not least, her pants were pulled down and he could see blood coming from between her thighs along with some bruising.

Yaseer rushed over to where his future laid out on the floor, got down on both knees, and cradled her in his arms.

"Paris, babe, wake up! I'm here. Baby, please wake up! Come on baby cakes, wake up, my queen! I need you!" Yaseer begged with tears falling from his eyes. "No, no, no, not my baby!" he pleaded.

"Fuck waiting on the ambulance," Yaseer thought as he picked Paris up in his arms and carried her to the car. He was going to take her to the hospital his damn self.

Yaseer sat next to Paris' bed with his head leaned back on the headrest of the chair that he was sitting in, hoping that his love would wake up soon. He felt like the biggest ass in America.

This shit was all my fuckin' fault, was one of the thoughts that kept circulating through Yaseer's head. So many thoughts were going through his head.

Damn, if it hadn't been for me fucking up, then Paris would have never even left me, let alone been in no hotel or laying up in this damn hospital, Yaseer thought to himself.

146

He knew that his girl was messed up badly. Every time he looked at her and saw the swelling in her face from some bastard putting his hands on her and breaking her nose and busting her mouth open, it got him vexed. Not only that, the doctor had confirmed that she had indeed been raped.

He was so pissed. Yaseer was seeing colors and stars at the same damn time. He was trained to go! Yaseer was ready for war with the fool that had the heart to come up against a real goon like himself.

Yaseer felt his heart splitting in two just from looking at her. At the same time, he was ready to body the person who was responsible for her lying in the hospital. He couldn't wait to murder the idiot who was even brave enough to lay a finger near his woman. Yaseer was in his own little world, thinking up different ways to kill the person responsible for the pain he was feeling when he heard his name being called. A rush of excitement rushed through his body, thinking that his baby could be awake. He was sure that he was dreaming.

"Yaseer" Paris called out.

Yaseer heard his name being called once again. He slowly opened his eyes, praying that this was not a cruel joke. He was shocked to see Paris looking back at him. You would have thought that he had just won the lottery, that's just how ecstatic he was at that time.

"Babe you're awake," Yaseer whispered, leaning down close to her and rubbing her hair.

Paris took a minute to take in her surroundings. After a moment, everything came rushing back to her at once. She saw images of what had happened to her. She remembered being in her hotel room and Yaseer's boy coming over. She also remembered him threatening her because she would not help him with his plan for Yaseer. She remembered him choking and raping her until she passed out from the pain and lack of oxygen. Paris looked over at Yaseer before responding to him in a soft voice.

"How long have I been in here?"

Yaseer looked down at the floor before bringing his eyes back to her face and answering her. "You have been in here for three days. You took some powerful blows and the doctor said that if you had been hit just a tad harder in the head you, would have died. Baby, I'm so, so sorry! I swear that I am. I promise that whoever did this to you will pay with their life. Do you have any idea about who did this to you?"

Paris turned her head. She was ashamed and afraid at the same time. Yaseer was the only man who could put an ounce of fear in her heart because she never wanted to lose him. Although she had left him, she had eventually planned to go back to him, kids and all. She just couldn't imagine life without him.

There was no way that she could tell him who had done this because she did not want him finding out that her father was the judge that had sentenced his parents. Her father was as crooked as they come. He had been taking money for years from kingpins, including Yaseer's father, until things started going sour between her dad and his, which was the reason he decided to make an example out of the Davis family.

"Paris, babe? Do you know who did this to you?" Yaseer repeated, drawing her out of her thoughts. Yaseer took his finger, put it under her chin and turned her face back to him. It broke his heart even more to see her crying. "Love, you have to tell me who did this to you. I need to know."

"I—I don't know Yaseer. He had on a mask but he spoke as though he knew you," Paris lied.

Yaseer's mind went into overdrive, trying to think of who would do this. One name popped in Yaseer's head but he refused to even dwell on it because there was no way it could be true. But then again, could it be so? His boy's face was the only one that kept recurring in his head. He hoped and prayed to God that it was not Kai'yan. But then again, how would Kai'yan have known anything when he didn't even have a clue that Paris had even left him. Yaseer needed answers.

"Babe, is there anything that was familiar about him?"

"No," was her response.

Yaseer knew she was lying because she started chewing on her inner cheek. Obviously, she had forgotten who her man was because if she hadn't, she would have known that she couldn't get a lie past him, even if she was a human lie detector.

He was becoming furious. Paris was lying to him, which only raised his suspicions more that it had to be someone close for her to even think about lying to him. He was ready to kill anybody who even looked like he wanted to jump stupid. Whoever this fool was, he had just signed his death certificate and had no clue he was about to be the most talked about death in history. Yaseer was about to deliver a fate that was so brutal not even DNA would be able to find out who the human remains belonged to.

"You a hundred percent certain that you don't know who did this to you?" Yaseer questioned her, trying to warn her in a subtle way that he had caught her in a lie.

"Yes, I am sure. Don't you think I would tell you? No, I don't know who it was," Paris stated with tears slowly falling out of her eyes.

"I love you," Yaseer responded before standing and walking out of the room. He couldn't get a handle on his anger or the pain that was in his heart and he only knew one way to numb the pain for a while. The streets were about to feel the heat of Yaseer Aleem Davis, starting with the person who he had a feeling was behind this.

Whoever was a part of this and whoever is trying to cause my downfall better have been getting right with their maker because I'm about to become their personal hell on earth. And Lord help Kai'yan if he had anything to do with any of this, Yaseer thought to himself.

The pain that he was about to cause his so-called family wouldn't be equivalent to the pain in his heart, but it would be damn close enough.

Time for war, Yaseer thought to himself.

He knew for sure if there was one snake, there was bound to be others. He just had to find out who was all in that den of snakes so that he could chop their heads off one by one.

Yaseer rushed out of the hospital as fast as he could, hopped in his car, and sped off. He felt like his blood was boiling. If anyone knew how much pain he could cause, it should be the ones close to him. He figured they must have needed a reminder to help show them who the real Boss was.

Chapter 13

Yaseer sat outside his brother's house debating rather to go in or not. He needed someone to talk to. It seemed like he couldn't catch a break.

Ever since Paris came home from jail over a month ago, things had constantly been happening. First there was the shooting. Then there was the incident of her receiving a note telling her to meet him at the wrong location, which led her to finding out about Chaunte and Madison. Now Paris was in the hospital because of some low-life putting his hands on her.

"What the fuck?" Yaseer screamed out in the confines of his car. Something was not right with all of this. As soon as Paris was well enough, Yaseer planned on calling a group meeting so he could see for himself who the trader was. He had the perfect plan to make whoever it was talk.

Yaseer decided he would see Liam another day. Right now, he couldn't even trust him because he was the one who was supposed to be meeting him at the restaurant, but instead Paris showed up in his place. Everybody was a suspect as of this moment. Yaseer started his car and made his way back to the hospital. When Yaseer got close to Paris' room, he saw his boy Ezra walking down the hallway.

"What up, son?" he said as he got closer to Yaseer and then dapped him up.

"Nothing right now. Some nigga done hurt my baby. They put their hands on my girl man."

"Damn! Why you ain't call me? When we going to ride out to go find and kill this fool?"

"Shit, I'm ready soon as I get my girl home. Hopefully, they will release her in the morning. Right now, I need to go be by her side. I think she know who did this to her but for some reason she lying to me. I will tell you what, as soon as I find out who did this, I promise I'm killing they whole family and saving their ass for last. That's on my momma," Yaseer stated, looking Ezra square in the eyes and walking off. He was a suspect, too.

Yaseer had only taken a couple of steps before he turned back around and called Ezra's name.

"Aye, Ezra. What brings you up here? Sorry for being rude. I was so busy talking about my problems that I didn't bother to make sure you were okay."

"My girl up here, she wasn't feeling well, been throwing up and shit. I made her ass come here and get checked out. I think she pregnant, but we will see. I'm on my way down to go run and get her something."

"Well congrats just in case I don't get to speak with you later on, and tell Melonie I said congrats." Yaseer turned back around and continued on to Paris' room. When Yaseer walked in, Paris all but jumped out of her skin.

"Yaseer, you scared the shit out of me."

"Damn, girl, who did you think was going to walk through that door other than me and the hospital staff? You look like you feel a little better than you did when I left out earlier."

"I don't know, maybe my sister or one of the crew members. And I do feel slightly better. I'm still sore but feeling better than when I first woke up."

"Well, I do need to tell you this, I have not called anyone to tell them what happened yet. I had to get myself together before telling them, but I just seen Ezra and told him. I am positive that he will tell everyone."

"You didn't tell my sister? She is going to flip the fuck out."

"Shit! Damn, I was so wrapped up in my emotions that I forgot that she was the one person I was supposed to call and tell. Fuck!" Yaseer pulled out his cell and called London. She was going to be beyond pissed. The phone rang two times before London picked up.

"Hello," she answered, sounding out of breath.

"Sup L, were you busy?"

"Nah, nah, what's up?"

"I'm sorry I'm just now telling you this and you have every right to be pissed, but three days ago when I went to Paris' hotel room to talk to her, I found her on the floor beaten badly and she had been raped as well. She is in the hospital right now. I'm sitting beside her. Before you go off, I was so wrapped up in my emotions that I didn't even think to call you and I apologize." Yaseer sat there waiting for her to respond. "London—London," he called her name in vain.

He pulled his phone away from his ear and looked at his phone. London had hung up on him and was more than likely on her way up to the hospital.

Not even fifteen minutes later, London was walking into the room. She mugged Yaseer and then ran to Paris' bedside.

"What the hell happened? Are you okay? Do you know who did it? I tell you what, let me catch that bastard and I promise it's a wrap." London was still going in when Liam, Kai'yan, and Brooklyn all walked in.

"Damn, sis, are you okay? London called on the way to tell me what happened and I called everyone else. I called E, but he said he was dealing with a family issue."

Everyone was bombarding Paris with questions and it looked as if she was getting a little overwhelmed. Yaseer was about to say something but Paris spoke up before he could say anything.

"Everyone! Everyone!" she called, bringing a halt to their questions. "I am ok, just very sore. And no, I don't know who did this. Now I do have a few requests. Kai'yan, can you hook a sista up with some Mickey D's? Yaseer, could you go to the house and get me something other than this hospital gown to put on? And bro-in-law, could you go to the Cheesecake Factory and get me a slice of cheese cake with strawberries on top?" Everyone nodded.

"I'm riding shotgun with you Liam,"

London declared.

"And I'm riding shotgun with you Kai'yan," Brooklyn announced.

"Well, damn! Ain't nobody wanna ride with ya boy?" Yaseer said and then looked at Brooklyn. *What the fuck she need to ride with Kai'yan for?* Yaseer thought to himself.

Until he knew who was doing what, she wasn't riding alone with no damn body. He'd be damned.

"Yo, Brook, come ride with yo big bruh."

"Yas, why the hell do you need me to ride with you to go scoop some clothes up?" Brooklyn questioned.

"Why in the hell do you need to ride with Kai'yan to get a burger?" Yaseer answered her question with a question.

"Maybe 'cause I want a damn burger, did that ever cross your mind? Yaseer, don't play with me. You know I plays no games with you. I ain't these other muhfuckas in the streets. I do as I damn well please."

Yaseer smiled and shook his head. Brooklyn just didn't know he was about ten seconds away from putting his foot up her Native American looking ass.

"You may not be them, but please don't be fooled that because you are grown that I still won't get in that ass because of yo smart ass mouth. Now I said ride with yo big bruh, end of discussion."

"Just ride with him Brook, it's no biggie. I will call you when I get there and you can just tell me what you want," Kai'yan said, looking at Yaseer with major attitude as he walked out of the room.

"I'm for damn sure not riding with you now after the way you just acted. I will stay here with Paris," Brooklyn said as she sat down in a chair next to Paris' bed.

Yaseer did not care about her being pissed, but she was not about to ride with Kai'yan until his name was cleared off of his suspect list, point blank period, end of discussion.

Yaseer didn't even respond. He walked over to Paris, kissed her on the forehead, and left out. Liam and London left out right behind him.

"Aye, bruh, we need to talk later on," Liam said. Then he sped up and walked past Yaseer with London hot on his heels.

Twenty minutes later, Liam and London were on their way back to the hospital, cheesecake in hand, when London turned her body toward Liam as much as the seat belt would allow her to and asked, "What the hell is going on with Yaseer today?"

"I don't know. I have never seen him act that way with Brooklyn. And quite frankly, I felt that it was petty."

"Yaseer is protective over her. For whatever reason, he didn't want her to ride with Kai'yan. I'm pretty sure that he had a reason. He always does."

"Why? Do you think he keeping something from us about Kai'yan that we don't know?" Liam asked.

"Nah, I was just curious as to why he went ham over her riding with him."

"You. Just curious. Fuck no! What the fuck on ya mind? Speak it ma, you know I hate when you say and ask shit and then leave me with cliffhangers, trying to figure shit out."

London let out a sigh. "Did he mention that he got any kind of information? It just feels like that would be the only reason for him to be acting funny style with Kai'yan. Then, on top of that, if Kai'yan is a snake, then why the fuck is Yas dragging his feet to bury this nigga? Normally we would have been bodied this nigga within a matter of hours. So if he feel this nigga fraudulent, then why the fuck this bitch still walking around breathing? Yo, he getting soft or something and I ain't feeling it."

Although Liam understood her reason for questioning how Yaseer was handling shit, he refused to question his brother because if he knew nothing else, he knew Yaseer had a damn plan and he obviously had a reason as to why he hasn't moved yet. He understood that Yaseer thought someone close was involved and that they couldn't move the same way being that this fool may know their moves. Questioning Yaseer's authority and movements was showing that your trust was starting to waver and when trust started to waver so did loyalty and respect, and that was unacceptable. Liam pulled over onto the shoulder of the road, shut the engine off, and turned to London.

"Don't you ever question how my brother's moving. If you got a problem with the way he handling shit, then hock that shit up and spit it out. Please don't make me start questioning your loyalty 'cause then we gon' have mad problems and that's that shit you don't want. End of discussion," Liam said with anger evident in his voice.

He started the car back up, pulled back into traffic, and continued on his way to Presbyterian Hospital. London sat there speechless. She couldn't believe the way he had just handled her. No one ever got away with handling her like that and he was the only one brave enough to do it.

The rest of the ride was quiet. Each of them was in their own thoughts. By the time they had gotten upstairs, everyone was there, including Ezra. Everyone sat and chopped it up until visitation was over.

Chapter 14

Two days later, Yaseer was finally able to take his girl home. He helped her into the house and upstairs to their bedroom and got her settled in bed to take a nap. Paris was still sore, but she was feeling a lot better. They both were ecstatic to be away from the hospital. Between the hospital staff and police, they never could get any rest. It felt good for them to be home. Every time Yaseer thought of why she was there in the first place, he got vexed and was ready to bust something. But in due time, he would have sweet revenge.

"You need me to get you anything?" Yaseer asked Paris.

"No, sweetie, all I need is for you to come lay down and hold me."

Yaseer walked over to the bed, got in, and gathered her up in his arms. "I love you, Paris. God knows I love you. I am so, so sorry for what that bastard has put you through. I can't imagine if I had not got to you in time. I'm dead without you. You know I will protect you with my life. I promise you he will get what is coming to him. I love you so much, my queen. Just hang in there with me, mi amor."

"Babe, trust me, I don't plan on leaving again. I should have never even went to go stay in a hotel. London had offered for me to kick it with her but I just wanted to be alone. I don't know what I was thinking. I was hurt and upset and I just needed some time to clear my head and pull myself together, Yaseer. I love you, but bae it is going to take time for my heart to heal from this. Just imagine if the shoe was on the other foot and you came home and found out that I had two children by another man. I wanted to be the one who gave birth to your first seed. It's going to take time for me to get used to, but I refuse to live without you. Know this though, the moment that bitch you got pregnant steps out of her lane, I'm beating the brakes off of her ass and that's on everything that I love. Hell, to think about it, I owe her an ass whoopin' now," Paris replied.

"Paris, baby, I will spend the rest of my life trying to prove how sorry I am for what I have done to hurt you. And I will spend the rest of my life showing you how much I love you and making up for the times I hurt you. I will never forgive myself for what has happened to you because of you loving me," Yaseer said on the brink of tears. He wasn't a punk or a weak man, but he was human. Yaseer always tried his hardest to not let that clear fluid fall from his eyes. But this was one time he couldn't control the tears that flowed down his face.

Paris lay cradled in Yaseer's arms staring at the ceiling reminiscing on when they first met. They'd grown up in the same neighborhood as well as went to school together. Back then Paris and London was living with her Aunt Londa. Her mom had dropped them off at her aunts and ran off with her new husband and didn't look back.

Paris and Yaseer met on her first day at Davidson middle school. He was one of the first kids at school who had started teasing her. However, Yaseer had met his match with Paris and they couldn't stand each other.

A year later, Yaseer happened to be walking home from school when he saw this boy harassing Paris. His first thought was, *It ain't none of his business. I'ma just keep on walking.* But when the guy went to lift his hand to hit Paris, Yaseer ran over and knocked the lil' nigga out cold. After that, Paris and Yaseer grew close.

By tenth grade they had officially started dating, but their relationship was cut short when Yaseer and his family ended up moving back New York and they lost contact. It was five and a half long years later before Yaseer moved back to Charlotte, North Carolina. And months longer before he ran into Paris again.

One of Yaseer's boys had invited him to a college party that the University of North Carolina

College was throwing. Later that night, he was talking to his mans when he saw a face that he had never forgotten.

Yaseer excused himself and made a beeline straight to her.

"Excuse me, beautiful, but can you tell me how much a flight to Paris will cost me?" Yaseer asked from behind her.

Paris spun around and collided with a face she had not seen in years. The only man she had ever loved and the only man that she had ever been with. She stood in shock for a moment before screaming and jumping into Yaseer's arms. Never in a million years had she thought she would see him again.

They ended up leaving the party early and had been together ever since.

Yaseer pulled Paris closer to his body, leaned down and kissed the top of her head. His mind was going a mile a minute. He loved Paris so much that it hurt, and he couldn't fathom life without her. All of her pain was because of him.

Yaseer made a promise to himself that this would be the last time she would cry tears of sorrow because of his actions. Next time they would be tears of happiness. After they talked for a little while longer, they both fell into a comfortable nap.

Three hours later, Yaseer was being awakened out of his sleep by a frantic scream from Paris.

Yaseer jumped up to see what was wrong. He looked over at Paris and saw the panic on her face as her phone slipped from her grasp. Immediately, he knew whatever she was about to tell him was not going to be good.

"What's wrong, bae?" Yaseer asked with grave concern.

"Brooklyn's been shot! We have to go now," she cried.

Yaseer tried his hardest to move so he could get up to go see about his sister but his body wouldn't move. "Not my sister, not my sister," he began to mumble to himself. "Fuck!" he bellowed then willed himself out of bed.

Yaseer threw on some clothes and grabbed his .45 off of the nightstand then went to the closet to get both of his .22's. He secured them in their proper places and was ready to roll.

Paris was on his heels. Before he knew it, they were damn near to the hospital.

"Shit!" Yaseer banged his hand against the dashboard as they sat at the light. "I didn't even apologize to her for spazzing out on her about riding with Kai'yan," he thought out loud.

As soon as the light turned green, he pressed the accelerator down and started bobbing and weaving, trying to get through downtown.

Yaseer hated downtown on the weekends, especially at nighttime because the roads were stupid busy.

"Yaseer," Paris called out.

"Yea," Yaseer responded, not really in the

mood to talk.

"Do you really think Kai'yan has anything to do with this? I saw the way you acted toward him when he came up to the hospital, which is something I have never seen you do with him."

"A few weeks ago, Ezra came to me with photos that showed Kai'yan in meetings and shit with this nigga named Kameron. Honestly, I have no clue if he has anything to do with it but I'm not ruling it out.

"H-how did Ezra get the photos?" Paris asked stuttering.

Yaseer glanced over at her. Something was off. She looked like she was scared for her life and in a daze.

"I don't know," was his response. Yaseer pressed his foot down on the gas and sped the rest of the way to the hospital.

He pulled in front of the hospital doors, put his car in park, hopped out, and gave his keys to the valet. Paris had already gotten out and was waiting on him. They walked into the hospital waiting room and saw the crew sitting there. They all looked as though they had been crying. Yaseer didn't know who was taking it the hardest Liam, or Kai'yan. Kai'yan was bawling, for real. But right now, Yaseer didn't care. Somebody was about to give him some answers.

"What the fuck happened?" he spat as he walked in.

Kai'yan looked up at him and Yaseer could honestly see the hurt in his face.

"Yaseer, I was at the store picking up some items for her. She told me to hold on for a split second while she answered her door. I heard her say *what up* to whoever was at the door and let them in. She was asking him did he want something to drink. He declined. She asked him what was his reason for stopping by. Then I heard her shout, *No, please don't shoot. Please, don't shoot me! Ezra nnooo!* I heard a shot ring out and then silence. I dropped the items I had in my hand and ran all the way to my car. I raced the whole way to her house. Why did he do this to her? Why? She didn't deserve this," Kai'yan cried out in his hands.

Yaseer's heart dropped. He looked over at Paris. She had her head hung low. His blood began to boil.

"You knew it was him and you didn't tell me? How the fuck could you let me continue to even be around him, knowing he was the one that put you in the hospital!? How in the hell could you keep your mouth shut on something like that!? Was you plotting with that nigga to kill me, huh? Answer me got damnit!"

Paris jumped up and was in his face so damn fast it looked like a damn Houdini trick.

"How the hell you gon' accuse me of plotting on you when I'm the one who been riding for you hard body? I'm the one who did your bid. I'm the one who sat behind bars every day while you ass was out here makin' fuckin' babies with two dollar strip hoes. I'm the one who was beaten

175

and raped because I wouldn't help him set you up. As a matter of fact, you are to blame for what happened to me because had you have warned me that you had fucked up before I even touched down, then maybe, just maybe I would not have even been in a hotel that night."

Paris paused before continuing on, all the while with tears streaming down her face. "I don't know how he knew where I was, but he did. Just like I don't know how he knew I was meeting you that day I received that note, but he did! The only reason I didn't inform you of who it was is because he threatened to kill my sister and I would rather have tried to take him down myself than to have put my sister in danger by telling you. If I were you, I wouldn't say shit else to me for the rest of the day, and save your sorry ass apology because I'm not trying to hear it." Paris said and then walked over to the chair farthest away from Yaseer to sit down.

Up until that moment, Liam was the only one who knew Yaseer had kids by another woman.

London had no clue why Paris had left Yaseer. She assumed that Paris had caught Yaseer creeping and Kai'yan definitely did not know, nor did anyone else.

Yaseer had so many emotions running through him. Just as he was about to say something, he saw the doctor coming down the hallway. Yaseer met him halfway.

"Are you Mr. Davis?" he asked.

"Yes, I am. How is she, Doc? Tell me she is going to be okay."

"Hello, my name is Dr. Barnett, and yes she has she pulled through the surgery just fine. She is very lucky to be alive. The bullet missed her heart by a few inches. Surprisingly, the baby pulled through, too. I'm highly shocked that she didn't miscarry," Dr. Barnett said.

Yaseer stood there speechless. *Brook pregnant by who?* She never even told him she was seeing someone. Everything else the doctor said, Yaseer didn't even hear. His mind was too far gone.

Then it hit Yaseer like a ton of bricks. Why was Kai'yan at the store for her when she could have called Liam or him to go for her? Yaseer wanted to go question Kai'yan about that. However, that could wait. They needed to come up with a way to get Ezra. One thing he knew was in order to get him like they wanted, they would have to play his little game.

Yaseer was about to show him, and any other nigga who wanted to play with a G like himself, how to really boss up.

Once Yaseer finished speaking with the doctor, he went back to the waiting room and notified his crew that they needed to have a meeting at The Chambers ASAP. They needed to come up with a plan to get Ezra and torture him in the worst way.

Yaseer also made a mental note to call his brother, Zyon, who still resided in New York so that he could tell him about Brooklyn. None of them left until after they were able to see Brooklyn, which wasn't until the next day.

Chapter 15

Good ole Monday rolled around. It had been two days since Brooklyn had been shot. She was finally awake and talking. She told Yaseer everything that she could before her pain medicine kicked in and sent her to sleep. So now Yaseer was sitting at the house waiting on Ezra to return his call. Yaseer purposely had blown his phone up texting and calling him about Brook so that Ezra wouldn't know that he was on to him. Yaseer should have gotten an Oscar for the way he had Ezra thinking that he suspected it was someone else.

"What a fuckin' dumb ass," Yaseer thought to himself. His phone started to vibrate on the table. He didn't even have to look at the caller I.D. to know it was Ezra calling. Yaseer swiped his thumb across the screen to accept the call.

"What up E?" Yaseer greeted.

"Ain't shit, how's Brooklyn?"

"You ain't shit and better than your ass

about to be," Yaseer thought. Trying his hardest to keep his thoughts in his head, he replied, "She still has not woken up yet. They have her on strong meds that keep her asleep so she doesn't have to feel the pain," Yaseer lied smoothly. He hated to lie. But at that moment, to get the revenge that he wanted, he had to keep Ezra thinking he was clueless.

"That's good, I'm glad to hear that."

Not as glad as I will be when my machete meets your neck, Yaseer pondered to himself.

Yaseer could just go ahead and kill him. But Ezra is far from dumb. He would expect Yaseer to try and kill him and no doubt would be well prepared. However, if the crew played like everything was good and had him thinking that they truly thought that it was someone else, then they could trap their Judas like they needed to, without a problem.

Yaseer started to tell Ezra to meet him at his house, but he needed a little more time before he could see him face to face without snapping his neck. He wanted Ezra to suffer in the worse way. He needed him to feel how he had been feeling.

"Thanks, bruh, by the way, we handling that nigga tomorrow so be ready," Yaseer said to him. *Ooohhh, I can't wait to be able to kill his ass. I am going to enjoy it. But, in a way, it is going to hurt me because I grew up with him and looked at him like a brother. But it is what it is,* he thought silently.

"A'ight, just hit me up, son, and I will be strapped and ready."

"I got ya. Matter of fact, just meet us at t\The Chambers tomorrow at 10PM, I will have him tied up and ready when you get there."

"A'ight, one," Ezra said.

*****

Ezra disconnected the call with Yaseer. *"Niggas are so stupid,"* Ezra thought to himself as he turned on his side and looked at Ariel.

"When do you plan on making your move, bae?" she asked him.

"Soon, you just worry about getting that nigga over here in your bed so I can catch him slippin' and finish Paris off. I would have went on and did it at the hospital but this way will hurt him more," Ezra said, all the while taking his hand and sliding it down to her hidden treasure.

Every time he fucked Yaseer's baby momma, it did something to him. Just to have what Yaseer once had made him feel like he was the shit because having something that Yaseer had made him feel like he could have anything. He couldn't stand Yaseer. The nigga always got what he wanted. Ever since he was little, he hated him. He envied the fact that Yaseer had the privilege of wearing name brand clothes and shoes. He despised the fact that Yaseer always had the latest gear and girls. Every time he looked up, Yaseer was bragging to him about what he got or what bad bitch he just fucked.

He also hated Yaseer because he was able to

experience having a two parent home. He envied that while he was at home getting beat day in and day out by his stepfather while his mother was out on the street doing drugs. He envied the fact that Yaseer had a loving home with parents who loved and adored him. He and Yaseer had the same dad. However, that was about to be the bombshell he would drop on Yaseer before he blew his brains to smithereens.

"I can't wait until you kill that little bitch of his. I nut every time I think about it," Ariel said as she removed Ezra's hand and climbed on top of him.

She couldn't stand the thought of Yaseer being with Paris over her. She thought that by carrying his children, eventually he would want to be with her instead of Paris. Hell, ole girl was in jail at the time so she made her move, hoping that by trapping him she could lock him down. Now she saw that removing Paris out of the picture completely was the only way that she could have

Yaseer completely. If she could not have him, Paris would not either, point blank, period. Once Ezra offed Paris, then she planned to off Ezra because there was no way in hell she was about to let him kill her boo. But until then, she was going to fuck the shit out of Ezra because his dick game was fucking A-1. She slid down onto Ezra's long, thick pole and began grinding slowly.

"Damn baby, that shit feel good," he said as he took his hands and placed them on her hips.

Ariel continued to ride up and down Ezra's steel, coming up right to the tip of his dick and then rolling her hips as she came down again and again.

"Aww, fuck," Ezra mumbled. Every time they fucked, she had him feeling like a straight bitch. He felt himself about to cum. "Turn over. I want your face down, ass up you know how I like it."

Ariel did as she was told.

Ezra smacked her ass as he positioned himself at her entrance and slid in nice and slow.

185

"Whose pussy is this?"

"It's yours."

"I can't hear you," was his response. Ezra was putting a mean hurting on Ariel's twatt.

"It's yours, Ezra. It's all yours, Daddy."

"You better not give my pussy to another nigga, you hear me? This my shit," Ezra said as he continued pounding away almost at his peak.

"Uuugghhh. That's right, daddy, fuck me hard," Ariel moaned out. He was pounding the hell out of her guts and man did it feel good.

"You gone help Daddy finish breaking that bitch nigga down?"

"Yyeesss," Ariel hissed between moans.

"You keep fucking with that nigga's head. I don't give a fuck how you doing it, long as the result is the same. Then we killing him, Paris, and everyone who fuck wit 'em the long way. You hear me, baby? Do it for us. I swear I'll wife you. Just do this for me," Ezra said.

"Okaaayyy, bbaaabbyy. I'ma ddooo iittt,"

Ariel responded.

"Good. Now cum on Daddy's dick."

Right on cue, Ariel came all over his steel. Ariel felt his member swell and become even harder. She knew he was just moments away from busting. She pulled away from him, bent down eye to eye level with his dick, and took him in her mouth.

Ezra groaned with pleasure.

"You like this shit, Daddy?" she said in between slurps.

"Hell yeah, you know I love this shit," Ezra moaned out and grabbed the back of Ariel's head to force her down further so she could deep throat him. Ariel caught the hint, relaxed her throat, and took him down her throat as far as he could go.

"Aaah aah shit. Damn. Fuck," Ezra swore as he bust long and hard down her throat.

Ariel sucked every last drop out. Then she sat up, licked her lips and leaned up to kiss him.

"Dam,n girl, your pussy good as hell, but

your head game is muhfuckin' lethal," Ezra said as he fell over to the side.

"Don't I know it? So when do you plan to kill Paris?" Ariel asked as she got up out of the bed.

"Tomorrow, but while I'm doing that, I need you working on Yaseer, getting him primed to be killed. I'm supposed to meet with him tomorrow. But if you play shit right, his ass will be kissing the ground before 10PM," Ezra said, getting up as well and throwing his clothes on.

"You're leaving?"

"Yea, I got to get shit mapped out for tomorrow," Ezra replied, grabbing his hoodie along with his phone and making his way to the door. "I'ma get at you tomorrow."

"A'ight, cool." Ariel shouted from the bathroom.

Ezra got in his car and cranked it up. "As soon as this bitch finish this shit, I got to dispose of her ass. What the fuck I look like marrying somebody? I'ma pimp 'til I die," Ezra mumbled and

Royal Nicole

then pulled off.

Chapter 16

Yaseer sat on the edge of the bed strapping up his boots and making sure all his gear was tight. Once he was finished, he sat back and eyed Paris as she got dressed.

"Come on, bae, we gotta hurry up so we can get over to the chambers and meet everyone."

"I'm coming, sweetie. I got to make sure I'm laced good. You know how I do. Paris put on thick black leggings, a black wife beater, her bulletproof vest, her black Timbs, and her gun holster, the one like the police wear, along with her twin nine millimeters stuck in their proper place. Then she threw on her black leather jacket, pulled her hair in a tight ponytail, and baby was TTG.

Yaseer got hard from seeing his baby getting G'd up and Trained To Go for her man.

"Baby, we move as one tonight. I need us all to make it out alive and unharmed tonight, okay."

"I know, sweetie. I love you."

"Love you, too," Yaseer replied.

Yaseer stood up to check himself out in the mirror one last time. He was decked out similar to Paris, except he had on black sweats and a skully.

They kissed each other then got in the car and left to go meet the crew. In less than two hours, Yaseer was going to officially kill the man that had been like a brother to him, his best friend, his traitor, his own personal Judas. Everything was already set in motion.

Ezra thought they were meeting at ten but that was only a ploy to make him think he had things under control. Yaseer planned to call him at seven and tell him they needed his assistance right away.

Yaseer looked over to his right at his strikingly beautiful gangstress, his ride or die. He made a promise to himself that no matter what he was going to wife her as soon as possible. He thought back on all the things that they had been through recently. Lord knows he was ready to put everything behind them so that they could move on.

Thirty minutes later, they were walking inside The Chambers. Everyone was there and ready to get things popping.

"What's good, bruh?" Liam said, dapping Yaseer up.

"Everything 'bout to be good after we take care of this Judas nigga."

"Hell the fuck yeah, my tool ready to spit that hot shit," Liam said to Yaseer as they turned to walk over to where Kai'yan was getting everything set up.

"You ready, bruh?" Yaseer asked when he got over to Kai'yan.

"As ready as I will ever be, now let's get me tied up before you call Judas," Kai'yan said, sitting down in the chair prepared to be strapped in. "Alright, I'm ready, let's get this party started. Who wants to take their first hit?"

"I will," Liam said then hauled off and punched Kai'yan in the face followed by another hit to the jaw.

"Damn, you hit soft, nigga," Kai'yan said, spitting out blood.

"Let me get some," Yaseer said and then punched Kai'yan right in the mouth.

"You been holding that one in, haven't you?" Kai'yan said, shaking his head and spitting out more blood.

"Maybe. Now two more hits will make it look more believable. Paris, London, come over here."

They had been standing off to the side quietly watching. They sashayed over to where the boys stood in front of Kai'yan.

"Who wants next?" Yaseer asked them.

"I do," London quickly volunteered. *Whap!* She pimp slapped the mess out of Kai'yan.

"Damn, shorty, you hit me like I just smashed and left," Kai'yan said.

It took a lot for him to feel pain so to him it was nothing to sit there and get hit.

"You wish. Your turn Paris," she said as she stepped back, giving Paris some space.

Paris didn't bother to say a word. She stepped directly in front of Kai'yan, stood and looked for a brief second over her shoulder, winked at Yaseer and then took her booted foot and kicked him dead in his mouth."

"Now I think that will make it look all the way believable," she said as she walked off.

Kai'yan was speechless. She had just busted his whole grill. He used his tongue to check for loose teeth then spit out a mouth full of blood.

Yaseer was in shock. That was the last thing he expected her to do. Yaseer quickly pulled himself together and picked up his phone to make the call to Ezra.

"Hello," Ezra answered.

"Aye, bruh, I need you to fall through right quick. You ain't gon' believe this shit," Yaseer said and then disconnected the call without even giving Ezra the time to respond.

"Shit!" Ezra spat out. "Damn!" He pushed speed dial. Two rings later he was connected to Ariel.

"Yeah," she said as she answered the call.

"Look, I got to go meet Yaseer right quick so I'm going to have to postpone on Paris to see what he needs and to make sure he not on our trail."

"Fuck. Alright, call me after you done with him," Ariel said, disconnecting the call. She rushed and threw on her Roca Wear jeans, a black baby tee, and some black and red J's. She had her own plans in her head.

"Fuck, Ezra!" she said out loud as she walked out of the door.

Ten minutes later, Ezra pulled up. He couldn't wait for Yaseer to die so he could take over his place and run it how he always thought it should have been ran from the get go.

Ezra got out and walked up to the door. As soon as he was about to punch in the access code, Yaseer pulled the door open.

"Come on, bruh, we been waiting on you," Yaseer said, stepping back so that Ezra could enter. "You were right about it being Kai'yan. Damn, I should have killed him after you told me, but I didn't want to accept that my best friend could betray me in such a manner. This nigga been doing all kind of bullshit behind my back like I wouldn't find out. Plus, some of Kameron's crew told me about the shit that Kam and Kai'yan used to be talking 'bout concerning me," Yaseer said, walking over to Door 6 where he had Kai'yan stationed.

Yaseer opened the door and walked over to Kai'yan. He pulled off the black pillow case they had over his head and clapped his hands.

"Wakey, wakey, lil' boy blue."

Kai'yan's face was fucked up. Ezra bent down eye to eye level with Kai'yan and then hocked spit in his face.

"I can't stand pussy niggas like you. I should put one right in the center of your head right now but that would be too easy," Ezra said, straightening back up his six foot frame.

"And I can't stand pussy niggas like you," Yaseer said and then hit Ezra in the back of his head with the butt off his gun, knocking him out cold.

"Get this fool strapped up to the muhfuckin' floor now," Yaseer said as he unlocked the restraints that held Kai'yan to the chair.

Kai'yan stood up strong and ready to put in work. Ezra was the man who had shot the love of his life and almost made her take her last breath on earth. He was in some pain, but not to the point where he couldn't take the time to stomp a mud hole in Ezra. He couldn't stand fraudulent people, male or female.

Yaseer watched as they secured his ex-best friend to the floor. Before he did anything, he just needed to know why. Why would Ezra do this to him? Yaseer loved him like family. He would have killed for him. Hell, he would have taken a bullet for him, and here Ezra had his bullets aiming for his head.

Yaseer walked over to the corner where he had a bucket of ice cold water sitting. He picked up the vessel and casually strolled back over to where Ezra was laid out at and threw the freezing liquid in his face.

Ezra gasped and tried to sit up to catch his breath.

"Hey, Sunshine, ready to get this show on the road?" Yaseer taunted. "Oh, a little advice, when shooting someone, be sure to aim for the head and check behind yourself for anything that could link you to the crime. For example, cell phones dumb ass. Now, before I get shit poppin' I have just one small question. Why?"

Ezra thought about lying but then decided fuck it he was about to die anyway.

"Because I hate you. I have never liked you. Every time I looked up yo ass was bragging about what and who you had. I should have been the one who had a nice house, new gear, girls, friends, and a loving family. That should have been me! But instead, you and them other three little bastards had every damn thing! You made the shit so easy. All I had to do was bug your shit and add a few tracking devices and boom I knew your every move. My favorite part is when Paris received the wrong note." Ezra chuckled. "All it took was a few big faces I paid to an old woman and the note was changed. You make me sick, and seeing you cry like a bitch made my day. "

"Nigga, we took you in and treated you like one of our own. We were your family, you stupid muthafucka," Yaseer shouted.

"You right about one thing, we are family. Let me tell you a little story, Mr. Perfect."

Once upon a time, there was a man who couldn't keep his dick in his pants. He met a woman by the name of Jahmina at his wife's birthday party that he threw for her, and boy did he find her attractive. She reminded him of a younger version of Pamela Grier. He approached her, they hit it off. So, they started fuckin' around unbeknownst to his wife who happened to be Jahmina's cousin. His wife had come to tell her cousin she was pregnant with her husband's first child.

Now, she had keys to her cousin's house so instead of knocking, she used her key to unlock the door. When she walked past the living room, she noticed a familiar jacket. Then as she continued to walk toward her cousin's room, she noticed more items: shoes, pants, boxers, and a shirt that she knew she had purchased months ago to celebrate her husband's birthday.

The closer she got, she started hearing moaning. She opened her cousin's door and there was her husband and cousin fuckin' missionary style with one of Jahmina's legs on his shoulder. He was steady pounding and neither of them noticed his wife was in the room until they heard a shot ring out in the room.

Later that year, this man's wife found out her cousin was carrying her husband's child. He never cheated again after that but it took a while for his wife's heart to heal afterwards.

The two cousins gave birth within a month of each other. Jahmina moved on with her life and met a guy named Tonio. They married, but the problem was he was an abusive alcoholic and she had become a junkie so that left their son in fucked up situations a lot of the time.

Now her child's father made sure they remained close so he could have contact with his son. Every time that little boy ended up with bruises and black eyes, he would go to his neighbor's house. After his mom killed his dad and was sent to jail, their neighbors adopted him and he lived there until his adopted parents were knocked by the jakes.

Later on, he found out his neighbors were really his dad and big cousin. His mom made sure he found out by letter after getting arrested. In case you haven't figured it out, I am not only your brother but we're cousins too. So yep, we family alright. Now the question is, was it really your dad's second in command who sent him and his wife to jail? Or was it a boy who was tired of him and his mother getting fucked over by a no good son of a bi—

"Shut up. Shut the fuck up. You a muhfuckin' lie! My dad would never not claim his child. Brooklyn could have told you that. Hell, she is the result of one of my dad's affairs, you fuckin' dumb ass."

"Let's handle this nigga so we can get the fuck out of here," Yaseer said. He bent over Ezra and said in a low voice, "Even if that were true, you should have told me that the moment you found out instead of having animosity with me over something that I could not control."

Yaseer balled up his fist and threw the first blow to Ezra's handsome face, then another, and then kept pounding and pounding Ezra's face until he was good and tired and could go no longer. Yaseer hated him for what he had done and the truth that he had just exposed. Yaseer stood up and stepped back with tears rolling down his face.

"Y'all turn," he said and then sat back and watched his crew stomp Ezra.

After two minutes of them constantly beating on him, Yaseer told them to stop and turn the jealous hearted fool over on his stomach. He still needed him conscious for what was about to happen next.

Yaseer walked over to where he was and just stood looking at Ezra for a quick second before opening his mouth to say anything.

"Your death will not be as easy because of the stunts your ass had pulled. Since you wanted to go around raping and shooting people, I got something for *your* ass. Bring them fools out here," Yaseer said to Paris.

She walked out for a split second and came back strutting with four crack head transvestites in tow. Ezra couldn't see what was going, but he knew something crazy was about to go down. He was scared shitless. Next thing he knew, he felt a blade slice through his jeans and boxers. He was completely assed out.

"Y'all know what to do, handle that. Then go holla at London and she will take care of y'all niggas," Yaseer stated while walking out of the room. This was the one thing he would not watch although he would enjoy hearing his bitch made screams.

At that point, Ezra started to figure out what was about to happen and wished that Yaseer would have just killed him.

The four transvestites walked over to Ezra.

"Oohh, Daddy, I heard you been having a real bad bitch fit so we are here to help calm you down," the first one said, bending over and rubbing Ezra's thigh.

Ezra squirmed and tried to break loose, but he knew it was no use in fighting it. The way Yaseer had The Chambers set up, it was basically impossible for anyone to breakout.

"It's 'bout to go down, Daddy," the tranny said.

Before he could think, he felt something being shoved inside of his anus. It felt like his body was being shattered like glass. He felt something trickling down his inner thigh. He would bet his last dollar that it was blood.

The first tranny was behind him, shoving his dick in and out of his ass. For the first time since he was a child, he began to cry. This was the sickest shit ever. He thought he was going to puke. One after another, they took turns raping him, taking his manhood.

Then, all off a sudden, he felt a worse pain and almost screamed his lungs out. His last rapist had cut off his family jewels. After that, Ezra blacked out. He could no longer take anymore.

The trannies walked out of the room, went to London, and all of them received eight balls. They immediately exited the premises so they could go chase that high.

Ezra was lying on the floor ass out with blood all around him. London went to feel for a pulse. He was still alive. Barely, but yet still alive. The Torture Crew all walked over to him, pulled their tools out, and riddled his body with bullets. Ezra's body looked like Swiss cheese after they got done. Then they went to work, dismembering his now damaged body.

"Get the cleanup crew in here to take this trash out of our establishment," Yaseer said, walking out of the room to his office to shower and grab a change of clothes so he could get Ezra's blood off of him.

Yaseer opened the door and couldn't believe his eyes. Ariel was sitting in there like she owned the place.

"How the fuck this bitch even know the code to get into my fuckin' office?" Yaseer pondered.

Then it clicked in his head and came rushing to him like a ton of bricks falling down on him from the sky. *These two nasty muthafuckas were in on this shit together,* he thought silently. However, he had no intentions of letting her know that he had figured the rest of the puzzle out.

"How the fuck you get in my office?" asked Yaseer.

"I have my ways. Now, look, you got two options, you can either leave Paris or I kill her," she said, standing up and walking toward him. "It's your choice, boo."

"Bitch, please, get the fuck out of here," Yaseer spat. "If you lay a finger on my girl, the coroner will scrape your ass up off the pavement. Fuck with this shit if you want to," he threatened.

Ariel squinted her eyes at him in anger. "You heard what I said," she uttered defiantly.

The thought of killing her right then crossed Yaseer's mind, but he decided he would rather torture her ass nice and slowly. Make her ass suffer for having the audacity to come at him with that dumb shit. "Do you really want to play hardball with me?" he posed. Ariel was about to reply when Yaseer cut her off. "Matter of fact, don't even answer that," he said. "Since you're *MJ bad*, let me

go get her for you and let you tell her yourself.
We'll see how the fuck that works out for you." He
moved pass her headed for the door. *Bitch about to
find out how Paris get down.*

As soon as Yaseer's hand touched the door
knob, Ariel brought out her knife and shoved the
blade into his back. He let out a surprised squeak.
"Tell your bitch this, nigga!" Ariel spat as she
stabbed him again and again with such quiet fury
that the attack was almost soundless.

With blood pouring down his back and
weakness encompassing him quickly, Yaseer spun
around and reached for Ariel's arm in a futile
attempt to thwart the onslaught but her hand was a
blur. The blade plunged into his chest and he
staggered back and sunk down to his knees, looking
up at her in disbelief as his vision grew fuzzy and
sudden darkness reached out for him as he slumped
down on his side, still as a chalk line at the scene of
a homicide.

Feeling no mercy, Ariel looked down at the

bloodiness at her feet and gritted derisively, "Boss up, nigga." She walked out of Yaseer's office feeling giddy. In her head, neither she nor Paris would have him. *Problem solved.*

She had almost reached the exit when she spotted Zyon heading in her direction. In spite of her anxiousness to get ghost, she couldn't stop herself from taking in his physique. That nigga reminded her of the actor Boris Kodjoe except he wasn't bald and his swagger was straight thuggish. *If I had the time,* Ariel thought as she continued to walk.

Zyon walked down the hallway on his way to find his brother. He had already notified him that he was coming down after he heard about Brooklyn getting shot.

He saw a beautiful woman walking his way. She looked like a real life version of Pocahontas. Shorty's hips were banging.

As she got closer, he began to notice blood on her clothes. Then he saw the blade in her hand.

He immediately became alert. He stopped in his tracks and looked Ariel in the eye. Neither of them blinked but Zyon's gun was out in a flash. "Who the fuck is you?"

"Hi," Ariel responded lamely and tried to keep it moving, but Zyon was not going for that shit.

"Don't move another step or I will splatter yo shit all over this fucking floor," he said as he aimed the gun at her pretty little head.

Ariel tightened her grip on the handle of her knife. Now it was her turn to Boss Up.

To Be Continued…

Boss'N Up II coming soon

ACKNOWLEDGMENTS

OMG! I cannot believe I am writing acknowledgments! This is one of the most exciting events in my life. Where do I begin?

First off, I would like to thank my Lord and Savior Jesus Christ, for giving me the gift to write.

I would like to give a huge shout out to my heartbeat, and the reason I stay hustling and on my grind, my own little personal angel, my daughter Neriah Krissett Dunlap. Mommy may fuss a lot but know that mommy loves you and just want you to be the best that you can be. I love you, sweetheart.

Thank you to my parents Tracsy Grady, Eugene H. Davis II, and Jeanette Davis for being my parents raising me, helping me when you could and showing your love and support.

Thank you to all my siblings: Ikia, Gene, Ongela, Shameer, Andrew, and Aaron. I love you all so much. Thank you for all that you do whether it be big or small. Shout outs to my nieces and nephews: Tyriek, Jayla, Serenity, Nevaeh aka Baby D, Brennar, Zaelyn, Kingston, Jaden, and Dorian Auntie loves you.

To my Uncle Benny, Mmmmaaannn I love you! You are one of the best uncle a girl could have. Your Honeydew is making it!

Much love to my Uncle Keith, Chucky, and Uncle Larry. To my Aunt Patty, Pam, Shirley, and Jackie love you.

To all my cousins it's too many of y'all to name, but just know I love you and thank you for everything and being who you are.

To Aunt Vikki, I love you to pieces. Oh, gosh! Thank you for all the times you have helped me and have been my shoulder to lean on, my friend and all. I can't thank you enough! Love you Mani, Kayla, Mikey, LeeLee, and Jalora aka LoLO love you too Ma dukes and Chucky.

To my close friends who have been my A1 since Day 1! David Banks, man, you know you my ninja, my man a hunnid grand throughout all that we have been through you have been there and we have survived almost 8 years of friendship. Wow! A long time, huh? Much love.

Aliyah, dang I remember us meeting in the guidance office. We was supposed to be a rap group LOL. Sade, oh do I remember the time we worked at Xtensions doing hair, us being pregnant together and all.

Koren, I remember meeting you at Garinger. You were my first friend there. Courtney, I swear you always keep me in line, but have me cracking up at the same time. Crystal, I remember meeting you at the G along with Koren and Raven, Christa, girrlll them middle and high school days, though a decade has already passed. And Evelyn, hahaha you were the one who told me I was pregnant with Neriah. Remember when I bet our whole training class at Sykes .50 cents that I wasn't pregnant? LOL. I LOVE YOU ALL! No matter how far I may live away from you all know that our friendship will never fail but instead continue to grow stronger.

To Rosco aka Sco. What's up, homie?

To the Sargents: Mrs. Gina, Mr. Dwayne, Kasey, Kristen, and Katina. Thank you for being there and having my back countless times, whether it was giving me a place to stay or watching Riah. I appreciate all that you do and have done.

To Latisha Lew Lew Lewinson, lawd, how many times have we stayed up talking late nights about any and everything; shedding tears and all? Thank you for always being there, being a true friend and never judging me. You always keep it 100 with me. I love you!

Lenika, heeyyy baabbyy! (N.O. voice) Girl you my homie. You real as they come! Thank you for being you.

Brandi, Giles, and Masterpiece. Thank you all for being there for me to talk to or to give me advice. To the TNB bosses Tonsie, Toni Doe, Stephanie, Kenya, Giles, Wynter, and Erica! Much Love. Thank you all for your love and support. You all were there when it all began! Lissha Sadler, thank you for all the times you have helped me out with this book.

SPECIAL SHOUT OUT TO CA$H The Boss man with the fire pen! THANK YOU THANK YOU THANK YOU for giving me this opportunity and for believing in me! I never thought I would ever be an author! Thank you for putting up with me and all my shenanigans. Love you, Boss man.

Special shout to NeNe Capri. Thank you for being there! To La'Tonya West, Aaron Bebo, Authoress Marie A. Norfleet, and Sabrina Eubanks. Thank you for paving the way for other authors. Sabrina, I swear you keep me rolling big sis! Norma, Rita, and Bernie Bagley

HEEEEYYYY!!!!! Shout to my label mates Tranay, Linnea, Coffee, Frank, J Peach, Lady Stiletto and Authoress Forever Redd. CAROLINAS STAND UP!

Special shout out to the editors and everyone who had something to do with this book!!! Shout out to Writing Royalty as well. And to

Bigmofrombflo.

To Mrs. Shica, if I can achieve my dream of writing a book so can you! Love you!

Momma Denise remember going to CP together and us teaching dance together those were the days. Love you!

Last but certainly not least, special shouts to my Grandma Marva and My Grandma Davis. I love you and you will always remain in my heart. R.I.P. I hope I make you proud.

To anyone else I may have forgotten, charge it to my head and not my heart. Know that I love you and if I didn't mention you this go around, I got you next time around. Much love and enjoy.

Coming Soon From Lock Down Publications

THE KING CARTEL

By **Frank Gresham**

BONDS OF DECEPTION

By **Lady Stiletto**

A DANGEROUS LOVE

By **J Peach**

LOVE KNOWS NO BOUNDARIES II

By **Coffee**

Available Now

LOVE KNOWS NO BOUNDARIES

By **Coffee**

SLEEPING IN HEAVEN, WAKING IN HELL

By **Forever Redd**

THE DEVIL WEARS TIMBS

By **Tranay Adams**

DON'T FU#K WITH MY HEART

By **Linnea**

Royal Nicole

BOOKS BY LDP'S CEO, CA$H

TRUST NO MAN

TRUST NO MAN 2

TRUST NO MAN 3

BONDED BY BLOOD

SHORTY GOT A THUG

A DIRTY SOUTH LOVE

THUGS CRY

THUGS CRY 2

TRUST NO BITCH

TRUST NO BITCH 2

TRUST NO BITCH 3

TIL MY CASKET DROPS

Coming Soon

TRUST NO BITCH (EYEZ' STORY)

THUGS CRY 3

BONDED BY BLOOD 2

Made in the USA
Coppell, TX
28 September 2020

38890242R00122